Classic Christmas Stories

A Collection of Favorite Holiday Stories

CRANBERRY CLASSICS

This compilation first published by Cranberry Classics 2022.

Cover Design by Legacy Marketing Services

Print: 978-1-953279-12-5
Hardcover: 978-1-953279-13-2
Ebook: 978-1-953279-14-9
Audiobook: 978-1-953279-15-6

Cranberry Classics
Houston, TX

An imprint of Efusion Media Group
www.efusionmg.com

Contents

A Christmas Carol

By George MacDonald

Babe Jesus lay in Mary's lap,
The sun shone in his hair;
And this was how she saw, mayhap,
The crown already there.

For she sang: "Sleep on, my little king;
Bad Herod dares not come;
Before thee sleeping, holy thing,
The wild winds would be dumb."

"I kiss thy hands, I kiss thy feet,
My child, so long desired;
Thy hands will never be soiled, my sweet;
Thy feet will never be tired."

"For thou art the king of men, my son;
Thy crown I see it plain!
And men shall worship thee, every one,
And cry, Glory! Amen!"

Babe Jesus he opened his eyes wide--
At Mary looked her lord.
Mother Mary stinted her song and sighed;
Babe Jesus said never a word.

The Gift of the Magi

By O. Henry

One dollar and eighty-seven cents. That was all. And sixty cents of it was in pennies. Pennies saved one and two at a time by bulldozing the grocer and the vegetable man and the butcher until one's cheeks burned with the silent imputation of parsimony that such close dealing implied. Three times Della counted it. One dollar and eighty-seven cents. And the next day would be Christmas.

There was clearly nothing to do but flop down on the shabby little couch and howl. So Della did it. Which instigates the moral reflection that life is made up of sobs, sniffles, and smiles, with sniffles predominating.

While the mistress of the home is gradually subsiding from the first stage to the second, take a look at the home. A furnished flat at $8 per week. It did not exactly beggar description, but it certainly had that word on the lookout for the mendicancy squad.

In the vestibule below was a letter-box into which no letter would go, and an electric button from which no mortal finger could coax a ring. Also appertaining thereunto was a card bearing the name "Mr. James Dillingham Young."

The "Dillingham" had been flung to the breeze during a former period of prosperity when its possessor was being paid $30 per week. Now, when the income was shrunk to $20, though, they were thinking seriously of contracting to a modest and unassuming D. But whenever Mr. James Dillingham Young came home and reached his flat above he was called "Jim" and greatly hugged by Mrs. James Dillingham Young, already introduced to you as Della. Which is all very good.

Della finished her cry and attended to her cheeks with the powder rag. She stood by the window and looked out dully at a gray cat walking a gray fence in a gray backyard. Tomorrow would be Christmas Day, and she had only $1.87 with which to buy Jim a present. She had been saving every penny she could for months, with this result. Twenty dollars a week doesn't go far. Expenses had been greater than she had calculated. They always are. Only $1.87 to buy a present for Jim. Her Jim. Many a happy hour she had spent planning for something nice for him. Something fine and rare and sterling—something just a little bit near to being worthy of the honor of being owned by Jim.

There was a pier glass between the windows of the room. Perhaps you have seen a pier glass in an $8 flat. A very thin and very agile person may, by observing his reflection in a rapid sequence of longitudinal strips, obtain a fairly accurate conception of his looks. Della, being slender, had mastered the art.

Suddenly she whirled from the window and stood before the glass. Her eyes were shining brilliantly, but her face had lost its color within twenty seconds.

Rapidly she pulled down her hair and let it fall to its full length.

Now, there were two possessions of the James Dillingham Youngs in which they both took a mighty pride. One was Jim's gold watch that had been his father's and his grandfather's. The other was Della's hair. Had the queen of Sheba lived in the flat across the airshaft, Della would have let her hair hang out the window some day to dry just to depreciate Her Majesty's jewels and gifts. Had King Solomon been the janitor, with all his treasures piled up in the basement, Jim would have pulled out his watch every time he passed, just to see him pluck at his beard from envy.

So now Della's beautiful hair fell about her rippling and shining like a cascade of brown waters. It reached below her knee and made itself almost a garment for her. And then she did it up again nervously and quickly. Once she faltered for a minute and stood still while a tear or two splashed on the worn red carpet.

On went her old brown jacket; on went her old brown hat. With a whirl of skirts and with the brilliant sparkle still in her eyes, she fluttered out the door and down the stairs to the street.

Where she stopped the sign read: "Mme. Sofronie. Hair Goods of All Kinds." One flight up Della ran, and collected herself, panting. Madame, large, too white, chilly, hardly looked the "Sofronie."

"Will you buy my hair?" asked Della.

"I buy hair," said Madame. "Take yer hat off and let's have a sight at the looks of it."

Down rippled the brown cascade.

"Twenty dollars," said Madame, lifting the mass with a practised hand.

"Give it to me quick," said Della.

Oh, and the next two hours tripped by on rosy wings. Forget the hashed metaphor. She was ransacking the stores for Jim's present.

She found it at last. It surely had been made for Jim and no one else. There was no other like it in any of the stores, and she had turned all of them inside out. It was a platinum fob chain simple and chaste in design, properly proclaiming its value by substance alone and not by meretricious ornamentation—as all good things should do. It was even worthy of The Watch. As soon as she saw it she knew that it must be Jim's. It was like him. Quietness and value—the description applied to both. Twenty-one dollars they took from her for it, and she hurried home with the 87 cents. With that chain on his watch Jim might be properly anxious about the time in any company. Grand as the watch was, he sometimes looked at it on the sly on account of the old leather strap that he used in place of a chain.

When Della reached home her intoxication gave way a little to prudence and reason. She got out her curling irons and lighted the gas and went to work repairing the ravages made by generosity added to love. Which is always a tremendous task, dear friends—a mammoth task.

Within forty minutes her head was covered with tiny, close-lying curls that made her look wonderfully like a truant schoolboy. She looked at her reflection in the mirror long, carefully, and critically.

"If Jim doesn't kill me," she said to herself, "before he takes a second look at me, he'll say I look like a Coney Island chorus girl. But what could I do—oh! what could I do with a dollar and eighty-seven cents?"

At 7 o'clock the coffee was made and the frying-pan was on the back of the stove hot and ready to cook the chops.

Jim was never late. Della doubled the fob chain in her hand and sat on the corner of the table near the door that he always entered. Then she heard his step on the stair away down on the first flight, and she turned white for just a moment. She had a habit of saying a little silent prayer about the simplest everyday things, and now she whispered: "Please God, make him think I am still pretty."

The door opened and Jim stepped in and closed it. He looked thin and very serious. Poor fellow, he was only twenty-two—and to be burdened with a family! He needed a new overcoat and he was without gloves.

Jim stopped inside the door, as immovable as a setter at the scent of quail. His eyes were fixed upon Della, and there was an expression in them that she could not read, and it terrified her. It was not anger, nor surprise, nor disapproval, nor horror, nor any of the sentiments that she had been prepared for. He simply stared at her fixedly with that peculiar expression on his face.

Della wriggled off the table and went for him.

"Jim, darling," she cried, "don't look at me that way. I had my hair cut off and sold because I couldn't have lived through Christmas without giving you a present. It'll grow out again—you won't mind, will you? I just had to do it. My hair grows awfully fast. Say 'Merry Christmas!' Jim, and let's be happy. You don't know what a nice—what a beautiful, nice gift I've got for you."

"You've cut off your hair?" asked Jim, laboriously, as if he had not arrived at that patent fact yet even after the hardest mental labor.

"Cut it off and sold it," said Della. "Don't you like me just as well, anyhow? I'm me without my hair, ain't I?"

Jim looked about the room curiously.

"You say your hair is gone?" he said, with an air almost of idiocy.

"You needn't look for it," said Della. "It's sold, I tell you—sold and gone, too. It's Christmas Eve, boy. Be good to me, for it went for you. Maybe the hairs of my head were numbered," she went on with sudden serious sweetness, "but nobody could ever count my love for you. Shall I put the chops on, Jim?"

Out of his trance Jim seemed quickly to wake. He enfolded his Della. For ten seconds let us regard with discreet scrutiny some inconsequential object in the other direction. Eight dollars a week or a million a year—what is the difference? A mathematician or a wit would give you the wrong answer. The magi brought valuable gifts, but that was not among them. This dark assertion will be illuminated later on.

Jim drew a package from his overcoat pocket and threw it upon the table.

"Don't make any mistake, Dell," he said, "about me. I don't think there's anything in the way of a haircut or a shave or a shampoo that could make me like my girl any less. But if you'll unwrap that package you may see why you had me going a while at first."

White fingers and nimble tore at the string and paper. And then an ecstatic scream of joy; and then, alas! a quick feminine change to hysterical tears and wails, necessitating the immediate employment of all the comforting powers of the lord of the flat.

For there lay The Combs—the set of combs, side and back, that Della had worshipped long in a Broadway window. Beautiful combs, pure tortoise shell, with jewelled rims—just the shade to wear in the beautiful vanished hair. They were expensive combs, she knew, and her heart had simply craved and yearned over them without the least hope of possession. And now, they were hers, but the tresses that should have adorned the coveted adornments were gone.

But she hugged them to her bosom, and at length she was able to look up with dim eyes and a smile and say: "My hair grows so fast, Jim!"

And then Della leaped up like a little singed cat and cried, "Oh, oh!"

Jim had not yet seen his beautiful present. She held it out to him eagerly upon her open palm. The dull precious metal seemed to flash with a reflection of her bright and ardent spirit.

"Isn't it a dandy, Jim? I hunted all over town to find it. You'll have to look at the time a hundred times a day now. Give me your watch. I want to see how it looks on it."

Instead of obeying, Jim tumbled down on the couch and put his hands under the back of his head and smiled.

"Dell," said he, "let's put our Christmas presents away and keep 'em a while. They're too nice to use just at present. I sold the watch to get the money to buy your combs. And now suppose you put the chops on."

The magi, as you know, were wise men—wonderfully wise men—who brought gifts to the Babe in the manger. They invented the art of giving Christmas presents. Being wise, their gifts were no doubt wise ones, possibly bearing the privilege of exchange in case of duplication. And here I have lamely related to you the uneventful chronicle of two foolish children in a flat who most unwisely sacrificed for each other the greatest treasures of their house. But in a last word to the wise of these days let it be said that of all who give gifts these two were the wisest. Of all who give and receive gifts, such as they are wisest. Everywhere they are wisest. They are the magi.

The Three Kings of Cologne

By John of Hildesheim,
adapted by H.S. Morris

A LEGEND OF THE MIDDLE AGES

Now, when the Children of Israel were gone out of Egypt, and had won and made subject to them Jerusalem and all the land lying about, there was in the Kingdom of Ind a tall hill called the Hill of Vaws, or the Hill of Victory. On this hill were stationed sentinels of Ind, who watched day and night against the Children of Israel, and afterward against the Romans.

And if an enemy approached, the keepers of the Hill of Vaws made a great fire to warn the inhabitants of the land so that the men might make ready to defend themselves.

Now in the time when Balaam prophesied of the Star that should betoken the birth of Christ, all the great lords and the people of Ind and in the East desired greatly to see this Star of which he spake; and they gave gifts to the keepers of the Hill of Vaws, and bade them, if they saw by night or by day any star in the air, that had not been seen aforetime, that they, the keepers, should send anon word to the people of Ind.

And thus was it that for so long a time the fame of this Star was borne throughout the lands of the East.

And the more the Star was sought for, and the more its fame increased, so much the more all the people of the Land of Ind desired to see it. So they ordained twelve of the wisest and greatest of the clerks of astronomy, that were in all that country about, and gave them great hire to keep watch upon the Hill of Vaws for the Star that was prophesied of Balaam.

Now, when Christ was born in Bethlehem of Judea, His Star began to rise in the manner of a sun, bright shining. It ascended above the Hill of Vaws, and all that day in the highest air it abode without moving, insomuch that when the sun was hot and most high there was no difference in shining betwixt them.

But when the day of the nativity was passed the Star ascended up into the firmament, and it had right many long streaks and beams, more burning and brighter than a brand of fire; and, as an eagle flying and beating the air with his wings, right so the streaks and beams of the Star stirred about.

Then all the people, both man and woman, of all that country about when they saw this marvelous Star, were full of wonder thereat; yet they knew well that it was the Star that was prophesied of Balaam, and long time was desired of all the people in that country.

Now, when the three worshipful kings, who at that time reigned in Ind, Chaldea, and Persia, were informed by the astronomers of this Star, they were right glad that they had grace to see the Star in their days.

Wherefore these three worshipful kings, Melchior, Balthazar, and Jasper (in the same hour the Star appeared to all three), though each of them was far from the other, and none knew of the others' purpose, decided to go and seek and worship the Lord and King of the Jews, that was new born, as the appearance of the Star announced.

So each king prepared great and rich gifts, and trains of mules, camels, and horses charged with treasure, and together with a great multitude of people they set forth on their journeys.

THE CHILD

Now, when these three worshipful kings were passed forth out of their kingdoms, the Star went before each king and his people. When they stood still and rested, the Star stood still; and when they went forward again, the Star always went before them in virtue and strength and gave light all the way.

And, as it is written, in the time that Christ was born, there was peace in all the world, wherefore in all the cities and towns through which they went there was no gate shut neither by night nor by day; and all the people of those same cities and towns marveled wonderfully as they saw kings and vast multitudes go by in great haste; but they knew not what they were, nor whence they came, nor whither they should go.

Furthermore these three kings rode forth over hills, waters, valleys, plains, and other divers and perilous places without hindrance, for all the way seemed to them plain and even. And they never took shelter by night nor by day, nor ever rested, nor did their horses and other beasts ever eat or drink till they had come to Bethlehem. And all this time it did seem to them as one day.

But when the three blessed kings had come near to Jerusalem, then a great cloud of darkness hid the Star from their sight. And when Melchior and his people were come fast by the city, they abode in fog and darkness. Then came Balthazar, and he abode under the same cloud near unto Melchior. Thereupon appeared Jasper with all his host.

So these three glorious kings, each with his host and burdens and beasts, met together in the highway without the city of Jerusalem. And, notwithstanding that none of them ever before had seen the other, nor knew him, nor had heard of his coming, yet at their meeting each one with great reverence and joy kissed the other. So afterward, when they had spoken together and each had told his purpose and the cause of his journey, they were much more glad and fervent. So they rode forth, and at the uprising of the sun, they came into Jerusalem. And yet the Star appeared not.

So then these three worshipful kings, when they were come into the city, asked of the people concerning the Child that was born; and when Herod heard this he was troubled and all Jerusalem with him, and he privately summoned to him these three kings and learned of them the time when the Star appeared. He then sent them forth, bidding them find the young Child and return to him.

Now when these three kings were passed out of Jerusalem the Star appeared to them again as it did erst, and went before them till they were come to Bethlehem.

Now, the nearer the kings came to the place where Christ was born, the brighter shined the Star, and they entered Bethlehem the sixth hour of the day. And they rode through the streets till they came before a little house. There the Star stood still, and then descended and shone with so great a light that the little house was full of radiance; till anon the Star went upward again into the air, and stood still always above the same place.

And the three kings went into the little house and found the Child with his mother, and they fell down and worshiped him, and offered him gifts.

And you shall understand that these three kings had brought great gifts from their own lands, rich ornaments and divers golden vessels, and many jewels and precious stones, and both gold and silver,—these they had brought to offer to the King of the Jews. But when they found the Lord in a little-house, in poor clothes, and when they saw that the Star gave so great and holy a light in all the place that it seemed as though they stood in a furnace of fire, then were they so sore afraid, that of all the rich jewels and ornaments they had brought with them, they chose from their treasures what came first to their hands. For Melchior took a round apple of gold in his hand, and thirty gilt pennies, and these he offered unto our Lord; and Balthazar took out of his treasury incense; and Jasper took out myrrh, and that he offered with weeping and tears.

And now after these three kings had worshiped the Lord, they abode in Bethlehem for a little space, and as they abode, there came a command to them, in their sleep, that they should not return to Herod; and so by another way they went home to their kingdoms. But the Star that had gone before appeared no more.

So these three kings, who had suddenly met together in the highway before Jerusalem, went home together with great joy and honor. And when, after many days' journey over perilous places, they had come to the Hill of Vaws, they made there a fair chapel in worship of the Child they had sought. Also they agreed to meet together at the same place once in the year, and they ordained that the Hill of Vaws should be the place of their burial.

So when the three worshipful kings had done what they would, they took leave of each other, and each one with his people rode to his own land rejoicing.

HOW THEY CAME TO COLOGNE

Now, after many years, a little before the feast of Christmas, there appeared a wonderful Star above the cities where these three kings dwelt, and they knew thereby that their time was come when they should pass from earth. Then with one consent they built, at the Hill of Vaws, a fair and large tomb, and there the three Holy Kings, Melchior, Balthazar, and Jasper died, and were buried in the same tomb by their sorrowing people.

Now after much time had passed away, Queen Helen, the mother of the Emperor Constantine, began to think greatly of the bodies of these three kings, and she arrayed herself, and, accompanied by many attendants, went into the Land of Ind.

And you shall understand that after she had found the bodies of Melchior, Balthazar, and Jasper, Queen Helen put them into one chest and ornamented it with great riches, and she brought them into Constantinople, with joy and reverence, and laid them in a church that is called Saint Sophia; and this church the Emperor Constantine did make,—he alone, with a little child, set up all the marble pillars thereof.

Now, after the death of the Emperor Constantine a persecution against the Christian faith arose, and in this persecution the bodies of the three worshipful kings were set at naught. Then came the Emperor Mauricius of Rome, and, through his counsel, the bodies of these three kings were carried to Italy, and there they were laid in a fair church in the city of Milan.

Then afterward, in the process of time, the city of Milan rebelled against the Emperor Frederick the First, and he, being sore beset, sent to Rainald, Archbishop of Cologne, asking for help.

This Archbishop with his army did take the city of Milan, and delivered it to the Emperor. And for this service did the Emperor grant, at the Archbishop's great entreaty, that he should carry forth to Cologne the bodies of the three blessed kings.

Then the Archbishop, with great solemnity and in procession, did carry forth from the city of Milan the bodies of the three kings, and brought them unto Cologne and there placed them in the fair church of Saint Peter. And all the people of the country roundabout, with all the reverence they might, received these relics, and there in the city of Cologne they are kept and beholden of all manner of nations unto this day.

Thus endeth the legend of these three blessed kings,—Melchior, Balthazar, and Jasper.

THE STORY OF THE OTHER WISE MAN

By Henry Van Dyke

Who seeks for heaven alone to save his soul,
May keep the path, but will not reach the goal;
While he who walks in love may wander far,
Yet God will bring him where the blessed are.

You know the story of the Three Wise Men of the East, and how they travelled from far away to offer their gifts at the manger-cradle in Bethlehem. But have you ever heard the story of the Other Wise Man, who also saw the star in its rising, and set out to follow it, yet did not arrive with his brethren in the presence of the young child Jesus? Of the great desire of this fourth pilgrim, and how it was denied, yet accomplished in the denial; of his many wanderings and the probations of his soul; of the long way of his seeking, and the strange way of his finding, the One whom he sought—I would tell the tale as I have heard fragments of it in the Hall of Dreams, in the palace of the Heart of Man.

THE SIGN IN THE SKY

In the days when Augustus Caesar was master of many kings and Herod reigned in Jerusalem, there lived in the city of Ecbatana, among the mountains of Persia, a certain man named Artaban, the Median. His house stood close to the outermost of the seven walls which encircled the royal treasury. From his roof he could look over the rising battlements of black and white and crimson and blue and red and silver and gold, to the hill where the summer palace of the Parthian emperors glittered like a jewel in a sevenfold crown.

Around the dwelling of Artaban spread a fair garden, a tangle of flowers and fruit-trees, watered by a score of streams descending from the slopes of Mount Orontes, and made musical by innumerable birds. But all colour was lost in the soft and odorous darkness of the late September night, and all sounds were hushed in the deep charm of its silence, save the plashing of the water, like a voice half sobbing and half laughing under the shadows. High above the trees a dim glow of light shone through the curtained arches of the upper chamber, where the master of the house was holding council with his friends.

He stood by the doorway to greet his guests—a tall, dark man of about forty years, with brilliant eyes set near together under his broad brow, and firm lines graven around his fine, thin lips; the brow of a dreamer and the mouth of a soldier, a man of sensitive feeling but inflexible will—one of those who, in whatever age they may live, are born for inward conflict and a life of quest.

His robe was of pure white wool, thrown over a tunic of silk; and a white, pointed cap, with long lapels at the sides, rested on his flowing black hair. It was the dress of the ancient priesthood of the Magi, called the fire-worshippers.

"Welcome!" he said, in his low, pleasant voice, as one after another entered the room—"welcome, Abdus; peace be with you, Rhodaspes and Tigranes, and with you my father, Abgarus. You are all welcome, and this house grows bright with the joy of your presence."

There were nine of the men, differing widely in age, but alike in the richness of their dress of many-coloured silks, and in the massive golden collars around their necks, marking them as Parthian nobles, and in the winged circles of gold resting upon their breasts, the sign of the followers of Zoroaster.

They took their places around a small black altar at the end of the room, where a tiny flame was burning. Artaban, standing beside it, and waving a barsom of thin tamarisk branches above the fire, fed it with dry sticks of pine and fragrant oils. Then he began the ancient chant of the Yasna, and the voices of his companions joined in the beautiful hymn to Ahura-Mazda:

We worship the Spirit Divine,
  all wisdom and goodness possessing,
Surrounded by Holy Immortals,
  the givers of bounty and blessing.
We joy in the works of His hands,
  His truth and His power confessing.
We praise all the things that are pure,
  for these are His only Creation;

The thoughts that are true, and the words
and deeds that have won approbation;
These are supported by Him,
and for these we make adoration.
Hear us, O Mazda! Thou livest
in truth and in heavenly gladness;
Cleanse us from falsehood, and keep us
from evil and bondage to badness;
Pour out the light and the joy of Thy life
on our darkness and sadness.
Shine on our gardens and fields,
Shine on our working and weaving;
Shine on the whole race of man,
Believing and unbelieving;
Shine on us now through the night,
Shine on us now in Thy might,
The flame of our holy love
and the song of our worship receiving.

The fire rose with the chant, throbbing as if it were made of musical flame, until it cast a bright illumination through the whole apartment, revealing its simplicity and splendour.

The floor was laid with tiles of dark blue veined with white; pilasters of twisted silver stood out against the blue walls; the clearstory of round-arched windows above them was hung with azure silk; the vaulted ceiling was a pavement of sapphires, like the body of heaven in its clearness, sown with silver stars. From the four corners of the roof hung four golden magic-wheels, called the tongues of the gods. At the eastern end, behind the altar, there were two dark-red pillars of porphyry; above them a lintel of the same stone, on which was carved the figure of a winged archer, with his arrow set to the string and his bow drawn.

The doorway between the pillars, which opened upon the terrace of the roof, was covered with a heavy curtain of the colour of a ripe pomegranate, embroidered with innumerable golden rays shooting upward from the floor. In effect the room was like a quiet, starry night, all azure and silver, flushed in the East with rosy promise of the dawn. It was, as the house of a man should be, an expression of the character and spirit of the master.

He turned to his friends when the song was ended, and invited them to be seated on the divan at the western end of the room.

"You have come to-night," said he, looking around the circle, "at my call, as the faithful scholars of Zoroaster, to renew your worship and rekindle your faith in the God of Purity, even as this fire has been rekindled on the altar. We worship not the fire, but Him of whom it is the chosen symbol, because it is the purest of all created things. It speaks to us of one who is Light and Truth. Is it not so, my father?"

"It is well said, my son," answered the venerable Abgarus. "The enlightened are never idolaters. They lift the veil of the form and go in to the shrine of the reality, and new light and truth are coming to them continually through the old symbols." "Hear me, then, my father and my friends," said Artaban, very quietly, "while I tell you of the new light and truth that have come to me through the most ancient of all signs. We have searched the secrets of nature together, and studied the healing virtues of water and fire and the plants. We have read also the books of prophecy in which the future is dimly foretold in words that are hard to understand. But the highest of all learning is the knowledge of the stars. To trace their courses is to untangle the threads of the mystery of life from the beginning to the end. If we could follow them perfectly, nothing would be hidden from us. But is not our knowledge of them still incomplete? Are there not many stars still beyond our horizon—lights that are known only to the dwellers in the far south-land, among the spice-trees of Punt and the gold mines of Ophir?"

There was a murmur of assent among the listeners.

"The stars," said Tigranes, "are the thoughts of the Eternal. They are numberless. But the thoughts of man can be counted, like the years of his life. The wisdom of the Magi is the greatest of all wisdoms on earth, because it knows its own ignorance. And that is the secret of power. We keep men always looking and waiting for a new sunrise. But we ourselves know that the darkness is equal to the light, and that the conflict between them will never be ended."

"That does not satisfy me," answered Artaban, "for, if the waiting must be endless, if there could be no fulfilment of it, then it would not be wisdom to look and wait. We should become like those new teachers of the Greeks, who say that there is no truth, and that the only wise men are those who spend their lives in discovering and exposing the lies that have been believed in the world. But the new sunrise will certainly dawn in the appointed time. Do not our own books tell us that this will come to pass, and that men will see the brightness of a great light?"

"That is true," said the voice of Abgarus;"every faithful disciple of Zoroaster knows the prophecy of the Avesta and carries the word in his heart. 'In that day Sosiosh the Victorious shall arise out of the number of the prophets in the east country. Around him shall shine a mighty brightness, and he shall make life everlasting, incorruptible, and immortal, and the dead shall rise again.'"

"This is a dark saying," said Tigranes, "and it may be that we shall never understand it. It is better to consider the things that are near at hand, and to increase the influence of the Magi in their own country, rather than to look for one who may be a stranger, and to whom we must resign our power."

The others seemed to approve these words. There was a silent feeling of agreement manifest among them; their looks responded with that indefinable expression which always follows when a speaker has uttered the thought that has been slumbering in the hearts of his listeners. But Artaban turned to Abgarus with a glow on his face, and said:

"My father, I have kept this prophecy in the secret place of my soul. Religion without a great hope would be like an altar without a living fire. And now the flame has burned more brightly, and by the light of it I have read other words which also have come from the fountain of Truth, and speak yet more clearly of the rising of the Victorious One in his brightness."

He drew from the breast of his tunic two small rolls of fine linen, with writing upon them, and unfolded them carefully upon his knee.

"In the years that are lost in the past, long before our fathers came into the land of Babylon, there were wise men in Chaldea, from whom the first of the Magi learned the secret of the heavens. And of these Balaam the son of Beor was one of the mightiest. Hear the words of his prophecy: 'There shall come a star out of Jacob, and a sceptre shall arise out of Israel.'"

The lips of Tigranes drew downward with contempt, as he said:

"Judah was a captive by the waters of Babylon, and the sons of Jacob were in bondage to our kings. The tribes of Israel are scattered through the mountains like lost sheep, and from the remnant that dwells in Judea under the yoke of Rome neither star nor sceptre shall arise."

"And yet," answered Artaban, "it was the Hebrew Daniel, the mighty searcher of dreams, the counsellor of kings, the wise Belteshazzar, who was most honored and beloved of our great King Cyrus. A prophet of sure things and a reader of the thoughts of God, Daniel proved himself to our people. And these are the words that he wrote." (Artaban read from the second roll:) "'Know, therefore, and understand that from the going forth of the commandment to restore Jerusalem, unto the Anointed One, the Prince, the time shall be seven and threescore and two weeks.'"

"But, my son," said Abgarus, doubtfully, "these are mystical numbers. Who can interpret them, or who can find the key that shall unlock their meaning?"

Artaban answered: "It has been shown to me and to my three companions among the Magi—Caspar, Melchior, and Balthazar. We have searched the ancient tablets of Chaldea and computed the time. It falls in this year. We have studied the sky, and in the spring of the year we saw two of the greatest stars draw near together in the sign of the Fish, which is the house of the Hebrews. We also saw a new star there, which shone for one night and then vanished. Now again the two great planets are meeting. This night is their conjunction. My three brothers are watching at the ancient temple of the Seven Spheres, at Borsippa, in Babylonia, and I am watching here. If the star shines again, they will wait ten days for me at the temple, and then we will set out together for Jerusalem, to see and worship the promised one who shall be born King of Israel. I believe the sign will come. I have made ready for the journey. I have sold my house and my possessions, and bought these three jewels—a sapphire, a ruby, and a pearl—to carry them as tribute to the King. And I ask you to go with me on the pilgrimage, that we may have joy together in finding the Prince who is worthy to be served."

While he was speaking he thrust his hand into the inmost fold of his girdle and drew out three great gems—one blue as a fragment of the night sky, one redder than a ray of sunrise, and one as pure as the peak of a snow mountain at twilight—and laid them on the outspread linen scrolls before him.

But his friends looked on with strange and alien eyes. A veil of doubt and mistrust came over their faces, like a fog creeping up from the marshes to hide the hills. They glanced at each other with looks of wonder and pity, as those who have listened to incredible sayings, the story of a wild vision, or the proposal of an impossible enterprise.

At last Tigranes said: "Artaban, this is a vain dream. It comes from too much looking upon the stars and the cherishing of lofty thoughts. It would be wiser to spend the time in gathering money for the new fire-temple at Chala. No king will ever rise from the broken race of Israel, and no end will ever come to the eternal strife of light and darkness. He who looks for it is a chaser of shadows. Farewell."

And another said: "Artaban, I have no knowledge of these things, and my office as guardian of the royal treasure binds me here. The quest is not for me. But if thou must follow it, fare thee well."

And another said: "In my house there sleeps a new bride, and I cannot leave her nor take her with me on this strange journey. This quest is not for me. But may thy steps be prospered wherever thou goest. So, farewell."

And another said: "I am ill and unfit for hardship, but there is a man among my servants whom I will send with thee when thou goest, to bring me word how thou farest."

But Abgarus, the oldest and the one who loved Artaban the best, lingered after the others had gone, and said, gravely: "My son, it may be that the light of truth is in this sign that has appeared in the skies, and then it will surely lead to the Prince and the mighty brightness. Or it may be that it is only a shadow of the light, as Tigranes has said, and then he who follows it will have only a long pilgrimage and an empty search. But it is better to follow even the shadow of the best than to remain content with the worst. And those who would see wonderful things must often be ready to travel alone. I am too old for this journey, but my heart shall be a companion of the pilgrimage day and night, and I shall know the end of thy quest. Go in peace."

So one by one they went out of the azure chamber with its silver stars, and Artaban was left in solitude.

He gathered up the jewels and replaced them in his girdle. For a long time he stood and watched the flame that flickered and sank upon the altar. Then he crossed the hall, lifted the heavy curtain, and passed out between the dull red pillars of porphyry to the terrace on the roof.

The shiver that thrills through the earth ere she rouses from her night sleep had already begun, and the cool wind that heralds the daybreak was drawing downward from the lofty snow-traced ravines of Mount Orontes. Birds, half awakened, crept and chirped among the rustling leaves, and the smell of ripened grapes came in brief wafts from the arbours.

Far over the eastern plain a white mist stretched like a lake. But where the distant peak of Zagros serrated the western horizon the sky was clear. Jupiter and Saturn rolled together like drops of lambent flame about to blend in one.

As Artaban watched them, behold, an azure spark was born out of the darkness beneath, rounding itself with purple splendours to a crimson sphere, and spiring upward through rays of saffron and orange into a point of white radiance. Tiny and infinitely remote, yet perfect in every part, it pulsated in the enormous vault as if the three jewels in the Magian's breast had mingled and been transformed into a living heart of light. He bowed his head. He covered his brow with his hands.

"It is the sign," he said. "The King is coming, and I will go to meet him."

BY THE WATERS OF BABYLON

All night long Vasda, the swiftest of Artaban's horses, had been waiting, saddled and bridled, in her stall, pawing the ground impatiently, and shaking her bit as if she shared the eagerness of her master's purpose, though she knew not its meaning.

Before the birds had fully roused to their strong, high, joyful chant of morning song, before the white mist had begun to lift lazily from the plain, the other wise man was in the saddle, riding swiftly along the high-road, which skirted the base of Mount Orontes, westward.

How close, how intimate is the comradeship between a man and his favourite horse on a long journey. It is a silent, comprehensive friendship, an intercourse beyond the need of words. They drink at the same way-side springs, and sleep under the same guardian stars. They are conscious together of the subduing spell of nightfall and the quickening joy of daybreak. The master shares his evening meal with his hungry companion, and feels the soft, moist lips caressing the palm of his hand as they close over the morsel of bread. In the gray dawn he is roused from his bivouac by the gentle stir of a warm, sweet breath over his sleeping face, and looks up into the eyes of his faithful fellow-traveller, ready and waiting for the toil of the day. Surely, unless he is a pagan and an unbeliever, by whatever name he calls upon his God, he will thank Him for this voiceless sympathy, this dumb affection, and his morning prayer will embrace a double blessing—God bless us both, and keep our feet from falling and our souls from death!

And then, through the keen morning air, the swift hoofs beat their spirited music along the road, keeping time to the pulsing of two hearts that are moved with the same eager desire—to conquer space, to devour the distance, to attain the goal of the journey.

Artaban must indeed ride wisely and well if he would keep the appointed hour with the other Magi; for the route was a hundred and fifty parasangs, and fifteen was the utmost that he could travel in a day. But he knew Vasda's strength, and pushed forward without anxiety, making the fixed distance every day, though he must travel late into the night, and in the morning long before sunrise.

He passed along the brown slopes of Mt. Orontes, furrowed by the rocky courses of a hundred torrents.

He crossed the level plains of the Nisaeans, where the famous herds of horses, feeding in the wide pastures, tossed their heads at Vasda's approach, and galloped away with a thunder of many hoofs, and flocks of wild birds rose suddenly from the swampy meadows, wheeling in great circles with a shining flutter of innumerable wings and shrill cries of surprise.

He traversed the fertile fields of Concabar, where the dust from the threshing-floors filled the air with a golden mist, half hiding the huge temple of Astarte with its four hundred pillars.

At Baghistan, among the rich gardens watered by fountains from the rock, he looked up at the mountain thrusting its immense rugged brow out over the road, and saw the figure of King Darius trampling upon his fallen foes, and the proud list of his wars and conquests graven high upon the face of the eternal cliff.

Over many a cold and desolate pass, crawling painfully across the wind-swept shoulders of the hills; down many a black mountain-gorge, where the river roared and raced before him like a savage guide; across many a smiling vale, with terraces of yellow limestone full of vines and fruit-trees; through the oak-groves of Carine and the dark Gates of Zagros, walled in by precipices; into the ancient city of Chala, where the people of Samaria had been kept in captivity long ago; and out again by the mighty portal, riven through the encircling hills, where he saw the image of the High Priest of the Magi sculptured on the wall of rock, with hand uplifted as if to bless the centuries of pilgrims; past the entrance of the narrow defile, filled from end to end with orchards of peaches and figs, through which the river Gyndes foamed down to meet him; over the broad rice-fields, where the autumnal vapours spread their deathly mists; following along the course of the river, under tremulous shadows of poplar and tamarind, among the lower hills; and out upon the flat plain, where the road ran straight as an arrow through the stubble-fields and parched meadows; past the city of Ctesiphon, where the Parthian emperors reigned, and the vast metropolis of Seleucia which Alexander built; across the swirling floods of Tigris and the many channels of Euphrates, flowing yellow through the corn-lands—Artaban pressed onward until he arrived, at nightfall of the tenth day, beneath the shattered walls of populous Babylon.

Vasda was almost spent, and he would gladly have turned into the city to find rest and refreshment for himself and for her. But he knew that it was three hours' journey yet to the Temple of the Seven Spheres, and he must reach the place by midnight if he would find his comrades waiting. So he did not halt, but rode steadily across the stubble-fields.

A grove of date-palms made an island of gloom in the pale yellow sea. As she passed into the shadow Vasda slackened her pace, and began to pick her way more carefully.

Near the farther end of the darkness an access of caution seemed to fall upon her. She scented some danger or difficulty; it was not in her heart to fly from it—only to be prepared for it, and to meet it wisely, as a good horse should do. The grove was close and silent as the tomb; not a leaf rustled, not a bird sang.

She felt her steps before her delicately, carrying her head low, and sighing now and then with apprehension. At last she gave a quick breath of anxiety and dismay, and stood stock-still, quivering in every muscle, before a dark object in the shadow of the last palm-tree.

Artaban dismounted. The dim starlight revealed the form of a man lying across the road. His humble dress and the outline of his haggard face showed that he was probably one of the poor Hebrew exiles who still dwelt in great numbers in the vicinity. His pallid skin, dry and yellow as parchment, bore the mark of the deadly fever which ravaged the marsh-lands in autumn. The chill of death was in his lean hand, and, as Artaban released it, the arm fell back inertly upon the motionless breast.

He turned away with a thought of pity, consigning the body to that strange burial which the Magians deem most fitting—the funeral of the desert, from which the kites and vultures rise on dark wings, and the beasts of prey slink furtively away, leaving only a heap of white bones in the sand.

But, as he turned, a long, faint, ghostly sigh came from the man's lips. The brown, bony fingers closed convulsively on the hem of the Magian's robe and held him fast.

Artaban's heart leaped to his throat, not with fear, but with a dumb resentment at the importunity of this blind delay. How could he stay here in the darkness to minister to a dying stranger? What claim had this unknown fragment of human life upon his compassion or his service? If he lingered but for an hour he could hardly reach Borsippa at the appointed time. His companions would think he had given up the journey. They would go without him. He would lose his quest.

But if he went on now, the man would surely die. If he stayed, life might be restored. His spirit throbbed and fluttered with the urgency of the crisis. Should he risk the great reward of his divine faith for the sake of a single deed of human love? Should he turn aside, if only for a moment, from the following of the star, to give a cup of cold water to a poor, perishing Hebrew?

"God of truth and purity," he prayed, "direct me in the holy path, the way of wisdom which Thou only knowest."

Then he turned back to the sick man. Loosening the grasp of his hand, he carried him to a little mound at the foot of the palm-tree. He unbound the thick folds of the turban and opened the garment above the sunken breast. He brought water from one of the small canals near by, and moistened the sufferer's brow and mouth. He mingled a draught of one of those simple but potent remedies which he carried always in his girdle—for the Magians were physicians as well as astrologers—and poured it slowly between the colourless lips. Hour after hour he labored as only a skilful healer of disease can do; and, at last, the man's strength returned; he sat up and looked about him.

"Who art thou?" he said, in the rude dialect of the country, "and why hast thou sought me here to bring back my life?"

"I am Artaban the Magian, of the city of Ecbatana, and I am going to Jerusalem in search of one who is to be born King of the Jews, a great Prince and Deliverer for all men. I dare not delay any longer upon my journey, for the caravan that has waited for me may depart without me. But see, here is all that I have left of bread and wine, and here is a potion of healing herbs. When thy strength is restored thou can'st find the dwellings of the Hebrews among the houses of Babylon."

The Jew raised his trembling hands solemnly to heaven.

"Now may the God of Abraham and Isaac and Jacob bless and prosper the journey of the merciful, and bring him in peace to his desired haven. But stay; I have nothing to give thee in return—only this: that I can tell thee where the Messiah must be sought. For our prophets have said that he should be born not in Jerusalem, but in Bethlehem of Judah. May the Lord bring thee in safety to that place, because thou hast had pity upon the sick."

It was already long past midnight. Artaban rode in haste, and Vasda, restored by the brief rest, ran eagerly through the silent plain and swam the channels of the river. She put forth the remnant of her strength, and fled over the ground like a gazelle.

But the first beam of the sun sent her shadow before her as she entered upon the final stadium of the journey, and the eyes of Artaban anxiously scanning the great mound of Nimrod and the Temple of the Seven Spheres, could discern no trace of his friends.

The many-coloured terraces of black and orange and red and yellow and green and blue and white, shattered by the convulsions of nature, and crumbling under the repeated blows of human violence, still glittered like a ruined rainbow in the morning light.

Artaban rode swiftly around the hill. He dismounted and climbed to the highest terrace, looking out towards the west.

The huge desolation of the marshes stretched away to the horizon and the border of the desert. Bitterns stood by the stagnant pools and jackals skulked through the low bushes; but there was no sign of the caravan of the wise men, far or near.

At the edge of the terrace he saw a little cairn of broken bricks, and under them a piece of parchment. He caught it up and read: "We have waited past the midnight, and can delay no longer. We go to find the King. Follow us across the desert." Artaban sat down upon the ground and covered his head in despair.

"How can I cross the desert," said he, "with no food and with a spent horse? I must return to Babylon, sell my sapphire, and buy a train of camels, and provision for the journey. I may never overtake my friends. Only God the merciful knows whether I shall not lose the sight of the King because I tarried to show mercy."

FOR THE SAKE OF A LITTLE CHILD

There was a silence in the Hall of Dreams, where I was listening to the story of the other wise man. And through this silence I saw, but very dimly, his figure passing over the dreary undulations of the desert, high upon the back of his camel, rocking steadily onward like a ship over the waves.

The land of death spread its cruel net around him. The stony wastes bore no fruit but briers and thorns. The dark ledges of rock thrust themselves above the surface here and there, like the bones of perished monsters. Arid and inhospitable mountain ranges rose before him, furrowed with dry channels of ancient torrents, white and ghastly as scars on the face of nature. Shifting hills of treacherous sand were heaped like tombs along the horizon. By day, the fierce heat pressed its intolerable burden on the quivering air; and no living creature moved, on the dumb, swooning earth, but tiny jerboas scuttling through the parched bushes, or lizards vanishing in the clefts of the rock. By night the jackals prowled and barked in the distance, and the lion made the black ravines echo with his hollow roaring, while a bitter, blighting chill followed the fever of the day. Through heat and cold, the Magian moved steadily onward.

Then I saw the gardens and orchards of Damascus, watered by the streams of Abana and Pharpar, with their sloping swards inlaid with bloom, and their thickets of myrrh and roses. I saw also the long, snowy ridge of Hermon, and the dark groves of cedars, and the valley of the Jordan, and the blue waters of the Lake of Galilee, and the fertile plain of Esdraelon, and the hills of Ephraim, and the highlands of Judah. Through all these I followed the figure of Artaban moving steadily onward, until he arrived at Bethlehem. And it was the third day after the three wise men had come to that place and had found Mary and Joseph, with the young child, Jesus, and had laid their gifts of gold and frankincense and myrrh at his feet.

Then the other wise man drew near, weary, but full of hope, bearing his ruby and his pearl to offer to the King. "For now at last," he said, "I shall surely find him, though it be alone, and later than my brethren. This is the place of which the Hebrew exile told me that the prophets had spoken, and here I shall behold the rising of the great light. But I must inquire about the visit of my brethren, and to what house the star directed them, and to whom they presented their tribute."

The streets of the village seemed to be deserted, and Artaban wondered whether the men had all gone up to the hill-pastures to bring down their sheep. From the open door of a low stone cottage he heard the sound of a woman's voice singing softly. He entered and found a young mother hushing her baby to rest. She told him of the strangers from the far East who had appeared in the village three days ago, and how they said that a star had guided them to the place where Joseph of Nazareth was lodging with his wife and her new-born child, and how they had paid reverence to the child and given him many rich gifts.

"But the travellers disappeared again," she continued, "as suddenly as they had come. We were afraid at the strangeness of their visit. We could not understand it. The man of Nazareth took the babe and his mother and fled away that same night secretly, and it was whispered that they were going far away to Egypt. Ever since, there has been a spell upon the village; something evil hangs over it. They say that the Roman soldiers are coming from Jerusalem to force a new tax from us, and the men have driven the flocks and herds far back among the hills, and hidden themselves to escape it."

Artaban listened to her gentle, timid speech, and the child in her arms looked up in his face and smiled, stretching out its rosy hands to grasp at the winged circle of gold on his breast. His heart warmed to the touch. It seemed like a greeting of love and trust to one who had journeyed long in loneliness and perplexity, fighting with his own doubts and fears, and following a light that was veiled in clouds.

"Might not this child have been the promised Prince?" he asked within himself, as he touched its soft cheek. "Kings have been born ere now in lowlier houses than this, and the favourite of the stars may rise even from a cottage. But it has not seemed good to the God of wisdom to reward my search so soon and so easily. The one whom I seek has gone before me; and now I must follow the King to Egypt."

The young mother laid the babe in its cradle, and rose to minister to the wants of the strange guest that fate had brought into her house. She set food before him, the plain fare of peasants, but willingly offered, and therefore full of refreshment for the soul as well as for the body. Artaban accepted it gratefully; and, as he ate, the child fell into a happy slumber, and murmured sweetly in its dreams, and a great peace filled the quiet room.

But suddenly there came the noise of a wild confusion and uproar in the streets of the village, a shrieking and wailing of women's voices, a clangor of brazen trumpets and a clashing of swords, and a desperate cry: "The soldiers! the soldiers of Herod! They are killing our children."

The young mother's face grew white with terror. She clasped her child to her bosom, and crouched motionless in the darkest corner of the room, covering him with the folds of her robe, lest he should wake and cry.

But Artaban went quickly and stood in the doorway of the house. His broad shoulders filled the portal from side to side, and the peak of his white cap all but touched the lintel.

The soldiers came hurrying down the street with bloody hands and dripping swords. At the sight of the stranger in his imposing dress they hesitated with surprise. The captain of the band approached the threshold to thrust him aside. But Artaban did not stir. His face was as calm as though he were watching the stars, and in his eyes there burned that steady radiance before which even the half-tamed hunting leopard shrinks, and the fierce bloodhound pauses in his leap. He held the soldier silently for an instant, and then said in a low voice:

"There is no one in this place but me, and I am waiting to give this jewel to the prudent captain who will leave me in peace."

He showed the ruby, glistening in the hollow of his hand like a great drop of blood.

The captain was amazed at the splendour of the gem. The pupils of his eyes expanded with desire, and the hard lines of greed wrinkled around his lips. He stretched out his hand and took the ruby.

"March on!" he cried to his men, "there is no child here. The house is still."

The clamour and the clang of arms passed down the street as the headlong fury of the chase sweeps by the secret covert where the trembling deer is hidden. Artaban re-entered the cottage. He turned his face to the east and prayed:

"God of truth, forgive my sin! I have said the thing that is not, to save the life of a child. And two of my gifts are gone. I have spent for man that which was meant for God. Shall I ever be worthy to see the face of the King?"

But the voice of the woman, weeping for joy in the shadow behind him, said very gently:

"Because thou hast saved the life of my little one, may the Lord bless thee and keep thee; the Lord make His face to shine upon thee and be gracious unto thee; the Lord lift up His countenance upon thee and give thee peace."

THE HIDDEN WAY OF SORROW

Then again there was a silence in the Hall of Dreams, deeper and more mysterious than the first interval, and I understood that the years of Artaban were flowing very swiftly under the stillness of that clinging fog, and I caught only a glimpse, here and there, of the river of his life shining through the shadows that concealed its course.

I saw him moving among the throngs of men in populous Egypt, seeking everywhere for traces of the household that had come down from Bethlehem, and finding them under the spreading sycamore-trees of Heliopolis, and beneath the walls of the Roman fortress of New Babylon beside the Nile—traces so faint and dim that they vanished before him continually, as footprints on the hard river-sand glisten for a moment with moisture and then disappear.

I saw him again at the foot of the pyramids, which lifted their sharp points into the intense saffron glow of the sunset sky, changeless monuments of the perishable glory and the imperishable hope of man. He looked up into the vast countenance of the crouching Sphinx and vainly tried to read the meaning of her calm eyes and smiling mouth. Was it, indeed, the mockery of all effort and all aspiration, as Tigranes had said—the cruel jest of a riddle that has no answer, a search that never can succeed? Or was there a touch of pity and encouragement in that inscrutable smile—a promise that even the defeated should attain a victory, and the disappointed should discover a prize, and the ignorant should be made wise, and the blind should see, and the wandering should come into the haven at last?

I saw him again in an obscure house of Alexandria, taking counsel with a Hebrew rabbi. The venerable man, bending over the rolls of parchment on which the prophecies of Israel were written, read aloud the pathetic words which foretold the sufferings of the promised Messiah—the despised and rejected of men, the man of sorrows and the acquaintance of grief.

"And remember, my son," said he, fixing his deep-set eyes upon the face of Artaban, "the King whom you are seeking is not to be found in a palace, nor among the rich and powerful. If the light of the world and the glory of Israel had been appointed to come with the greatness of earthly splendour, it must have appeared long ago. For no son of Abraham will ever again rival the power which Joseph had in the palaces of Egypt, or the magnificence of Solomon throned between the lions in Jerusalem. But the light for which the world is waiting is a new light, the glory that shall rise out of patient and triumphant suffering. And the kingdom which is to be established forever is a new kingdom, the royalty of perfect and unconquerable love. I do not know how this shall come to pass, nor how the turbulent kings and peoples of earth shall be brought to acknowledge the Messiah and pay homage to him. But this I know. Those who seek Him will do well to look among the poor and the lowly, the sorrowful and the oppressed."

So I saw the other wise man again and again, travelling from place to place, and searching among the people of the dispersion, with whom the little family from Bethlehem might, perhaps, have found a refuge. He passed through countries where famine lay heavy upon the land, and the poor were crying for bread. He made his dwelling in plague-stricken cities where the sick were languishing in the bitter companionship of helpless misery. He visited the oppressed and the afflicted in the gloom of subterranean prisons, and the crowded wretchedness of slave-markets, and the weary toil of galley-ships. In all this populous and intricate world of anguish, though he found none to worship, he found many to help. He fed the hungry, and clothed the naked, and healed the sick, and comforted the captive; and his years went by more swiftly than the weaver's shuttle that flashes back and forth through the loom while the web grows and the invisible pattern is completed.

It seemed almost as if he had forgotten his quest. But once I saw him for a moment as he stood alone at sunrise, waiting at the gate of a Roman prison. He had taken from a secret resting-place in his bosom the pearl, the last of his jewels. As he looked at it, a mellower lustre, a soft and iridescent light, full of shifting gleams of azure and rose, trembled upon its surface. It seemed to have absorbed some reflection of the colours of the lost sapphire and ruby. So the profound, secret purpose of a noble life draws into itself the memories of past joy and past sorrow. All that has helped it, all that has hindered it, is transfused by a subtle magic into its very essence. It becomes more luminous and precious the longer it is carried close to the warmth of the beating heart. Then, at last, while I was thinking of this pearl, and of its meaning, I heard the end of the story of the other wise man.

A PEARL OF GREAT PRICE

Three-and-thirty years of the life of Artaban had passed away, and he was still a pilgrim and a seeker after light. His hair, once darker than the cliffs of Zagros, was now white as the wintry snow that covered them. His eyes, that once flashed like flames of fire, were dull as embers smouldering among the ashes.

Worn and weary and ready to die, but still looking for the King, he had come for the last time to Jerusalem. He had often visited the holy city before, and had searched through all its lanes and crowded hovels and black prisons without finding any trace of the family of Nazarenes who had fled from Bethlehem long ago. But now it seemed as if he must make one more effort, and something whispered in his heart that, at last, he might succeed. It was the season of the Passover. The city was thronged with strangers. The children of Israel, scattered in far lands all over the world, had returned to the Temple for the great feast, and there had been a confusion of tongues in the narrow streets for many days.

But on this day there was a singular agitation visible in the multitude. The sky was veiled with a portentous gloom, and currents of excitement seemed to flash through the crowd like the thrill which shakes the forest on the eve of a storm. A secret tide was sweeping them all one way. The clatter of sandals, and the soft, thick sound of thousands of bare feet shuffling over the stones, flowed unceasingly along the street that leads to the Damascus gate.

Artaban joined company with a group of people from his own country, Parthian Jews who had come up to keep the Passover, and inquired of them the cause of the tumult, and where they were going.

"We are going," they answered, "to the place called Golgotha, outside the city walls, where there is to be an execution. Have you not heard what has happened? Two famous robbers are to be crucified, and with them another, called Jesus of Nazareth, a man who has done many wonderful works among the people, so that they love him greatly. But the priests and elders have said that he must die, because he gave himself out to be the Son of God. And Pilate has sent him to the cross because he said that he was the 'King of the Jews.'"

How strangely these familiar words fell upon the tired heart of Artaban! They had led him for a lifetime over land and sea. And now they came to him darkly and mysteriously like a message of despair. The King had arisen, but he had been denied and cast out. He was about to perish. Perhaps he was already dying. Could it be the same who had been born in Bethlehem, thirty-three years ago, at whose birth the star had appeared in heaven, and of whose coming the prophets had spoken?

Artaban's heart beat unsteadily with that troubled, doubtful apprehension which is the excitement of old age. But he said within himself, "The ways of God are stranger than the thoughts of men, and it may be that I shall find the King, at last, in the hands of His enemies, and shall come in time to offer my pearl for His ransom before He dies."

So the old man followed the multitude with slow and painful steps towards the Damascus gate of the city. Just beyond the entrance of the guard-house a troop of Macedonian soldiers came down the street, dragging a young girl with torn dress and dishevelled hair. As the Magian paused to look at her with compassion, she broke suddenly from the hands of her tormentors, and threw herself at his feet, clasping him around the knees. She had seen his white cap and the winged circle on his breast.

"Have pity on me," she cried, "and save me, for the sake of the God of Purity! I also am a daughter of the true religion which is taught by the Magi. My father was a merchant of Parthia, but he is dead, and I am seized for his debts to be sold as a slave. Save me from worse than death!"

Artaban trembled.

It was the old conflict in his soul, which had come to him in the palm-grove of Babylon and in the cottage at Bethlehem—the conflict between the expectation of faith and the impulse of love. Twice the gift which he had consecrated to the worship of religion had been drawn from his hand to the service of humanity. This was the third trial, the ultimate probation, the final and irrevocable choice.

Was it his great opportunity, or his last temptation? He could not tell. One thing only was clear in the darkness of his mind—it was inevitable. And does not the inevitable come from God?

One thing only was sure to his divided heart—to rescue this helpless girl would be a true deed of love. And is not love the light of the soul?

He took the pearl from his bosom. Never had it seemed so luminous, so radiant, so full of tender, living lustre. He laid it in the hand of the slave.

"This is thy ransom, daughter! It is the last of my treasures which I kept for the King."

While he spoke the darkness of the sky thickened, and shuddering tremors ran through the earth, heaving convulsively like the breast of one who struggles with mighty grief.

The walls of the houses rocked to and fro. Stones were loosened and crashed into the street. Dust clouds filled the air. The soldiers fled in terror, reeling like drunken men. But Artaban and the girl whom he had ransomed crouched helpless beneath the wall of the Praetorium.

What had he to fear? What had he to live for? He had given away the last remnant of his tribute for the King. He had parted with the last hope of finding Him. The quest was over, and it had failed. But, even in that thought, accepted and embraced, there was peace. It was not resignation. It was not submission. It was something more profound and searching. He knew that all was well, because he had done the best that he could, from day to day. He had been true to the light that had been given to him. He had looked for more.

And if he had not found it, if a failure was all that came out of his life, doubtless that was the best that was possible. He had not seen the revelation of "life everlasting, incorruptible and immortal." But he knew that even if he could live his earthly life over again, it could not be otherwise than it had been.

One more lingering pulsation of the earthquake quivered through the ground. A heavy tile, shaken from the roof, fell and struck the old man on the temple. He lay breathless and pale, with his gray head resting on the young girl's shoulder, and the blood trickling from the wound. As she bent over him, fearing that he was dead, there came a voice through the twilight, very small and still, like music sounding from a distance, in which the notes are clear but the words are lost. The girl turned to see if some one had spoken from the window above them, but she saw no one.

Then the old man's lips began to move, as if in answer, and she heard him say in the Parthian tongue:

"Not so, my Lord! For when saw I thee an hungered, and fed thee? Or thirsty, and gave thee drink? When saw I thee a stranger, and took thee in? Or naked, and clothed thee? When saw I thee sick or in prison, and came unto thee? Three-and-thirty years have I looked for thee; but I have never seen thy face, nor ministered to thee, my King."

He ceased, and the sweet voice came again. And again the maid heard it, very faintly and far away. But now it seemed as though she understood the words:

"Verily I say unto thee, inasmuch as thou hast done it unto one of the least of these my brethren, thou hast done it unto me."

A calm radiance of wonder and joy lighted the pale face of Artaban like the first ray of dawn on a snowy mountain-peak. One long, last breath of relief exhaled gently from his lips.

His journey was ended. His treasures were accepted. The other Wise Man had found the King.

Christmas Storms and Sunshine

Elizbeth Gaspell

In the town of——(no matter where) there circulated two local newspapers (no matter when). Now the *Flying Post* was long established and respectable—alias bigoted and Tory; the *Examiner* was spirited and intelligent—alias new-fangled and democratic. Every week these newspapers contained articles abusing each other; as cross and peppery as articles could be, and evidently the production of irritated minds, although they seemed to have one stereotyped commencement,—"Though the article appearing in last week's *Post* (or *Examiner*) is below contempt, yet we have been induced," &c., &c., and every Saturday the Radical shopkeepers shook hands together, and agreed that the *Post* was done for, by the slashing, clever *Examiner*; while the more dignified Tories began by regretting that Johnson should think that low paper, only read by a few of the vulgar, worth wasting his wit upon; however the *Examiner* was at its last gasp.

It was not though. It lived and flourished; at least it paid its way, as one of the heroes of my story could tell. He was chief compositor, or whatever title may be given to the head-man of the mechanical part of a newspaper. He hardly confined himself to that department. Once or twice, unknown to the editor, when the manuscript had fallen short, he had filled up the vacant space by compositions of his own; announcements of a forthcoming crop of green peas in December; a grey thrush having been seen, or a white hare, or such interesting phenomena; invented for the occasion, I must confess; but what of that? His wife always knew when to expect a little specimen of her husband's literary talent by a peculiar cough, which served as prelude; and, judging from this encouraging sign, and the high-pitched and emphatic voice in which he read them, she was inclined to think, that an "Ode to an early Rose-bud," in the corner devoted to original poetry, and a letter in the correspondence department, signed "Pro Bono Publico," were her husband's writing, and to hold up her head accordingly.

I never could find out what it was that occasioned the Hodgsons to lodge in the same house as the Jenkinses. Jenkins held the same office in the Tory paper as Hodgson did in the *Examiner*, and, as I said before, I leave you to give it a name. But Jenkins had a proper sense of his position, and a proper reverence for all in authority, from the king down to the editor and sub-editor. He would as soon have thought of borrowing the king's crown for a nightcap, or the king's sceptre for a walking-stick, as he would have thought of filling up any spare corner with any production of his own; and I think it would have even added to his contempt of Hodgson (if that were possible), had he known of the "productions of his brain," as the latter fondly alluded to the paragraphs he inserted, when speaking to his wife.

Jenkins had his wife too. Wives were wanting to finish the completeness of the quarrel, which existed one memorable Christmas week, some dozen years ago, between the two neighbours, the two compositors. And with wives, it was a very pretty, a very complete quarrel. To make the opposing parties still more equal, still more well-matched, if the Hodgsons had a baby ("such a baby!—a poor, puny little thing"), Mrs. Jenkins had a cat ("such a cat! a great, nasty, miowling tom-cat, that was always stealing the milk put by for little Angel's supper"). And now, having matched Greek with Greek, I must proceed to the tug of war. It was the day before Christmas; such a cold east wind! such an inky sky! such a blue-black look in people's faces, as they were driven out more than usual, to complete their purchases for the next day's festival.

Before leaving home that morning, Jenkins had given some money to his wife to buy the next day's dinner.

"My dear, I wish for turkey and sausages. It may be a weakness, but I own I am partial to sausages. My deceased mother was. Such tastes are hereditary. As to the sweets—whether plum-pudding or mince-pies—I leave such considerations to you; I only beg you not to mind expense. Christmas comes but once a year."

And again he had called out from the bottom of the first flight of stairs, just close to the Hodgsons' door ("such ostentatiousness," as Mrs. Hodgson observed), "You will not forget the sausages, my dear?"

"I should have liked to have had something above common, Mary," said Hodgson, as they too made their plans for the next day, "but I think roast beef must do for us. You see, love, we've a family."

"Only one, Jem! I don't want more than roast beef, though, I'm sure. Before I went to service, mother and me would have thought roast beef a very fine dinner."

"Well, let's settle it then, roast beef and a plum-pudding; and now, good-by. Mind and take care of little Tom. I thought he was a bit hoarse this morning."

And off he went to his work.

Now, it was a good while since Mrs. Jenkins and Mrs. Hodgson had spoken to each other, although they were quite as much in possession of the knowledge of events and opinions as though they did. Mary knew that Mrs. Jenkins despised her for not having a real lace cap, which Mrs. Jenkins had; and for having been a servant, which Mrs. Jenkins had not; and the little occasional pinchings which the Hodgsons were obliged to resort to, to make both ends meet, would have been very patiently endured by Mary, if she had not winced under Mrs. Jenkins's knowledge of such economy. But she had her revenge. She had a child, and Mrs. Jenkins had none. To have had a child, even such a puny baby as little Tom, Mrs. Jenkins would have worn commonest caps, and cleaned grates, and drudged her fingers to the bone. The great unspoken disappointment of her life soured her temper, and turned her thoughts inward, and made her morbid and selfish.

"Hang that cat! he's been stealing again! he's gnawed the cold mutton in his nasty mouth till it's not fit to set before a Christian; and I've nothing else for Jem's dinner. But I'll give it him now I've caught him, that I will!"

So saying, Mary Hodgson caught up her husband's Sunday cane, and despite pussy's cries and scratches, she gave him such a beating as she hoped might cure him of his thievish propensities; when lo! and behold, Mrs. Jenkins stood at the door with a face of bitter wrath.

"Aren't you ashamed of yourself, ma'am, to abuse a poor dumb animal, ma'am, as knows no better than to take food when he sees it, ma'am? He only follows the nature which God has given, ma'am; and it's a pity your nature, ma'am, which I've heard, is of the stingy saving species, does not make you shut your cupboard-door a little closer. There is such a thing as law for brute animals. I'll ask Mr. Jenkins, but I don't think them Radicals has done away with that law yet, for all their Reform Bill, ma'am. My poor precious love of a Tommy, is he hurt? and is his leg broke for taking a mouthful of scraps, as most people would give away to a beggar,—if he'd take 'em?" wound up Mrs. Jenkins, casting a contemptuous look on the remnant of a scrag end of mutton.

Mary felt very angry and very guilty. For she really pitied the poor limping animal as he crept up to his mistress, and there lay down to bemoan himself; she wished she had not beaten him so hard, for it certainly was her own careless way of never shutting the cupboard-door that had tempted him to his fault. But the sneer at her little bit of mutton turned her penitence to fresh wrath, and she shut the door in Mrs. Jenkins's face, as she stood caressing her cat in the lobby, with such a bang, that it wakened little Tom, and he began to cry.

Everything was to go wrong with Mary to-day. Now baby was awake, who was to take her husband's dinner to the office? She took the child in her arms, and tried to hush him off to sleep again, and as she sung she cried, she could hardly tell why,—a sort of reaction from her violent angry feelings. She wished she had never beaten the poor cat; she wondered if his leg was really broken. What would her mother say if she knew how cross and cruel her little Mary was getting? If she should live to beat her child in one of her angry fits?

It was of no use lullabying while she sobbed so; it must be given up, and she must just carry her baby in her arms, and take him with her to the office, for it was long past dinner-time. So she pared the mutton carefully, although by so doing she reduced the meat to an infinitesimal quantity, and taking the baked potatoes out of the oven, she popped them piping hot into her basket with the et-cæteras of plate, butter, salt, and knife and fork.

It was, indeed, a bitter wind. She bent against it as she ran, and the flakes of snow were sharp and cutting as ice. Baby cried all the way, though she cuddled him up in her shawl. Then her husband had made his appetite up for a potato pie, and (literary man as he was) his body got so much the better of his mind, that he looked rather black at the cold mutton. Mary had no appetite for her own dinner when she arrived at home again. So, after she had tried to feed baby, and he had fretfully refused to take his bread and milk, she laid him down as usual on his quilt, surrounded by playthings, while she sided away, and chopped suet for the next day's pudding. Early in the afternoon a parcel came, done up first in brown paper, then in such a white, grass-bleached, sweet-smelling towel, and a note from her dear, dear mother; in which quaint writing she endeavoured to tell her daughter that she was not forgotten at Christmas time; but that learning that Farmer Burton was killing his pig, she had made interest for some of his famous pork, out of which she had manufactured some sausages, and flavoured them just as Mary used to like when she lived at home.

"Dear, dear mother!" said Mary to herself. "There never was any one like her for remembering other folk. What rare sausages she used to make! Home things have a smack with 'em, no bought things can ever have. Set them up with their sausages! I've a notion if Mrs. Jenkins had ever tasted mother's she'd have no fancy for them town-made things Fanny took in just now."

And so she went on thinking about home, till the smiles and the dimples came out again at the remembrance of that pretty cottage, which would look green even now in the depth of winter, with its pyracanthus, and its holly-bushes, and the great Portugal laurel that was her mother's pride. And the back path through the orchard to Farmer Burton's; how well she remembered it. The bushels of unripe apples she had picked up there, and distributed among his pigs, till he had scolded her for giving them so much green trash.

She was interrupted—her baby (I call him a baby, because his father and mother did, and because he was so little of his age, but I rather think he was eighteen months old,) had fallen asleep some time before among his playthings; an uneasy, restless sleep; but of which Mary had been thankful, as his morning's nap had been too short, and as she was so busy. But now he began to make such a strange crowing noise, just like a chair drawn heavily and gratingly along a kitchen-floor! His eyes were open, but expressive of nothing but pain.

"Mother's darling!" said Mary, in terror, lifting him up. "Baby, try not to make that noise. Hush, hush, darling; what hurts him?" But the noise came worse and worse.

"Fanny! Fanny!" Mary called in mortal fright, for her baby was almost black with his gasping breath, and she had no one to ask for aid or sympathy but her landlady's daughter, a little girl of twelve or thirteen, who attended to the house in her mother's absence, as daily cook in gentlemen's families. Fanny was more especially considered the attendant of the upstairs lodgers (who paid for the use of the kitchen, "for

Jenkins could not abide the smell of meat cooking"), but just now she was fortunately sitting at her afternoon's work of darning stockings, and hearing Mrs. Hodgson's cry of terror, she ran to her sitting-room, and understood the case at a glance.

"He's got the croup! Oh, Mrs. Hodgson, he'll die as sure as fate. Little brother had it, and he died in no time. The doctor said he could do nothing for him—it had gone too far. He said if we'd put him in a warm bath at first, it might have saved him; but, bless you! he was never half so bad as your baby." Unconsciously there mingled in her statement some of a child's love of producing an effect; but the increasing danger was clear enough.

"Oh, my baby! my baby! Oh, love, love! don't look so ill; I cannot bear it. And my fire so low! There, I was thinking of home, and picking currants, and never minding the fire. Oh, Fanny! what is the fire like in the kitchen? Speak."

"Mother told me to screw it up, and throw some slack on as soon as Mrs. Jenkins had done with it, and so I did. It's very low and black. But, oh, Mrs. Hodgson! let me run for the doctor—I cannot abear to hear him, it's so like little brother."

Through her streaming tears Mary motioned her to go; and trembling, sinking, sick at heart, she laid her boy in his cradle, and ran to fill her kettle.

Mrs. Jenkins, having cooked her husband's snug little dinner, to which he came home; having told him her story of pussy's beating, at which he was justly and dignifiedly indignant, saying it was all of a piece with that abusive *Examiner*; having received the sausages, and turkey, and mince pies, which her husband had ordered; and cleaned up the room, and prepared everything for tea, and coaxed and duly bemoaned her cat (who had pretty nearly forgotten his beating, but very much enjoyed the petting), having done all these and many other things, Mrs. Jenkins sate down to get up the real lace cap. Every thread was pulled out separately, and carefully stretched: when, what was that? Outside, in the street, a chorus of piping children's voices sang the old carol she had heard a hundred times in the days of her youth:—

"As Joseph was a walking he heard an angel sing,
'This night shall be born our heavenly King.
He neither shall be born in housen nor in hall,
Nor in the place of Paradise, but in an ox's stall.
He neither shall be clothed in purple nor in pall,
But all in fair linen, as were babies all:
He neither shall be rocked in silver nor in gold,
But in a wooden cradle that rocks on the mould,'" &c.

She got up and went to the window. There, below, stood the group of grey black little figures, relieved against the snow, which now enveloped everything. "For old sake's sake," as she phrased it, she counted out a halfpenny apiece for the singers, out of the copper bag, and threw them down below.

The room had become chilly while she had been counting out and throwing down her money, so she stirred her already glowing fire, and sat down right before it—but not to stretch her lace; like Mary Hodgson, she began to think over long-past days, on softening remembrances of the dead and gone, on words long forgotten, on holy stories heard at her mother's knee.

"I cannot think what's come over me to-night," said she, half aloud, recovering herself by the sound of her own voice from her train of thought—"My head goes wandering on them old times. I'm sure more texts have come into my head with thinking on my mother within this last half hour, than I've thought on for years and years. I hope I'm not going to die. Folks say, thinking too much on the dead betokens we're going to join 'em; I should be loth to go just yet—such a fine turkey as we've got for dinner to-morrow, too!"

Knock, knock, knock, at the door, as fast as knuckles could go. And then, as if the comer could not wait, the door was opened, and Mary Hodgson stood there as white as death.

"Mrs. Jenkins!—oh, your kettle is boiling, thank God! Let me have the water for my baby, for the love of God! He's got croup, and is dying!"

Mrs. Jenkins turned on her chair with a wooden inflexible look on her face, that (between ourselves) her husband knew and dreaded for all his pompous dignity.

"I'm sorry I can't oblige you, ma'am; my kettle is wanted for my husband's tea. Don't be afeared, Tommy, Mrs. Hodgson won't venture to intrude herself where she's not desired. You'd better send for the doctor, ma'am, instead of wasting your time in wringing your hands, ma'am—my kettle is engaged."

Mary clasped her hands together with passionate force, but spoke no word of entreaty to that wooden face—that sharp, determined voice; but, as she turned away, she prayed for strength to bear the coming trial, and strength to forgive Mrs. Jenkins.

Mrs. Jenkins watched her go away meekly, as one who has no hope, and then she turned upon herself as sharply as she ever did on any one else.

"What a brute I am, Lord forgive me! What's my husband's tea to a baby's life? In croup, too, where time is everything. You crabbed old vixen, you!—any one may know you never had a child!"

She was down stairs (kettle in hand) before she had finished her self-upbraiding; and when in Mrs. Hodgson's room, she rejected all thanks (Mary had not the voice for many words), saying, stiffly, "I do it for the poor babby's sake, ma'am, hoping he may live to have mercy to poor dumb beasts, if he does forget to lock his cupboards."

But she did everything, and more than Mary, with her young inexperience, could have thought of. She prepared the warm bath, and tried it with her husband's own thermometer (Mr. Jenkins was as punctual as clockwork in noting down the temperature of every day). She let his mother place her baby in the tub, still preserving the same rigid, affronted aspect, and then she went upstairs without a word. Mary longed to ask her to stay, but dared not; though, when she left the room, the tears chased each other down her cheeks faster than ever. Poor young mother! how she counted the minutes till the doctor should come. But, before he came, down again stalked Mrs. Jenkins, with something in her hand.

"I've seen many of these croup-fits, which, I take it, you've not, ma'am. Mustard plaisters is very sovereign, put on the throat; I've been up and made one, ma'am, and, by your leave, I'll put it on the poor little fellow."

Mary could not speak, but she signed her grateful assent.

It began to smart while they still kept silence; and he looked up to his mother as if seeking courage from her looks to bear the stinging pain; but she was softly crying, to see him suffer, and her want of courage reacted upon him, and he began to sob aloud. Instantly Mrs. Jenkins's apron was up, hiding her face: "Peep-bo, baby," said she, as merrily as she could. His little face brightened, and his mother having once got the cue, the two women kept the little fellow amused, until his plaister had taken effect.

"He's better,—oh, Mrs. Jenkins, look at his eyes! how different! And he breathes quite softly——"

As Mary spoke thus, the doctor entered. He examined his patient. Baby was really better.

"It has been a sharp attack, but the remedies you have applied have been worth all the Pharmacopœia an hour later.—I shall send a powder," &c. &c.

Mrs. Jenkins stayed to hear this opinion; and (her heart wonderfully more easy) was going to leave the room, when Mary seized her hand and kissed it; she could not speak her gratitude.

Mrs. Jenkins looked affronted and awkward, and as if she must go upstairs and wash her hand directly.

But, in spite of these sour looks, she came softly down an hour or so afterwards to see how baby was.

The little gentleman slept well after the fright he had given his friends; and on Christmas morning, when Mary awoke and looked at the sweet little pale face lying on her arm, she could hardly realize the danger he had been in.

When she came down (later than usual), she found the household in a commotion. What do you think had happened? Why, pussy had been a traitor to his best friend, and eaten up some of Mr. Jenkins's own especial sausages; and gnawed and tumbled the rest so, that they were not fit to be eaten! There were no bounds to that cat's appetite! he would have eaten his own father if he had been tender enough. And now Mrs. Jenkins stormed and cried—"Hang the cat!"

Christmas Day, too! and all the shops shut! "What was turkey without sausages?" gruffly asked Mr. Jenkins.

"Oh, Jem!" whispered Mary, "hearken what a piece of work he's making about sausages,—I should like to take Mrs. Jenkins up some of mother's; they're twice as good as bought sausages."

"I see no objection, my dear. Sausages do not involve intimacies, else his politics are what I can no ways respect."

"But, oh, Jem, if you had seen her last night about baby! I'm sure she may scold me for ever, and I'll not answer. I'd even make her cat welcome to the sausages." The tears gathered to Mary's eyes as she kissed her boy.

"Better take 'em upstairs, my dear, and give them to the cat's mistress." And Jem chuckled at his saying.

Mary put them on a plate, but still she loitered.

"What must I say, Jem? I never know."

"Say—I hope you'll accept of these sausages, as my mother—no, that's not grammar;—say what comes uppermost, Mary, it will be sure to be right."

So Mary carried them upstairs and knocked at the door; and when told to "come in," she looked very red, but went up to Mrs. Jenkins, saying, "Please take these. Mother made them." And was away before an answer could be given.

Just as Hodgson was ready to go to church, Mrs. Jenkins came downstairs, and called Fanny. In a minute, the latter entered the Hodgsons' room, and delivered Mr. and Mrs. Jenkins's compliments, and they would be particular glad if Mr. and Mrs. Hodgson would eat their dinner with them.

"And carry baby upstairs in a shawl, be sure," added Mrs. Jenkins's voice in the passage, close to the door, whither she had followed her messenger. There was no discussing the matter, with the certainty of every word being overheard.

Mary looked anxiously at her husband. She remembered his saying he did not approve of Mr. Jenkins's politics.

"Do you think it would do for baby?" asked he.

"Oh, yes," answered she, eagerly;"I would wrap him up so warm."

"And I've got our room up to sixty-five already, for all it's so frosty," added the voice outside.

Now, how do you think they settled the matter? The very best way in the world. Mr. and Mrs. Jenkins came down into the Hodgsons' room, and dined there. Turkey at the top, roast beef at the bottom, sausages at one side, potatoes at the other. Second course, plum-pudding at the top, and mince pies at the bottom.

And after dinner, Mrs. Jenkins would have baby on her knee; and he seemed quite to take to her; she declared he was admiring the real lace on her cap, but Mary thought (though she did not say so) that he was pleased by her kind looks and coaxing words. Then he was wrapped up and carried carefully upstairs to tea, in Mrs. Jenkins's room. And after tea, Mrs. Jenkins, and Mary, and her husband, found out each other's mutual liking for music, and sat singing old glees and catches, till I don't know what o'clock, without one word of politics or newspapers.

Before they parted, Mary had coaxed pussy on to her knee; for Mrs. Jenkins would not part with baby, who was sleeping on her lap.

"When you're busy, bring him to me. Do, now, it will be a real favour. I know you must have a deal to do, with another coming; let him come up to me. I'll take the greatest of cares of him; pretty darling, how sweet he looks when he's asleep!"

When the couples were once more alone, the husbands unburdened their minds to their wives.

Mr. Jenkins said to his—"Do you know, Burgess tried to make me believe Hodgson was such a fool as to put paragraphs into the *Examiner* now and then; but I see he knows his place, and has got too much sense to do any such thing."

Hodgson said—"Mary, love, I almost fancy from Jenkins's way of speaking (so much civiler than I expected), he guesses I wrote that 'Pro Bono' and the 'Rose-bud,'—at any rate, I've no objection to your naming it, if the subject should come uppermost; I should like him to know I'm a literary man."

Well! I've ended my tale; I hope you don't think it too long; but, before I go, just let me say one thing.

If any of you have any quarrels, or misunderstandings, or coolnesses, or cold shoulders, or shynesses, or tiffs, or miffs, or huffs, with any one else, just make friends before Christmas,—you will be so much merrier if you do.

I ask it of you for the sake of that old angelic song, heard so many years ago by the shepherds, keeping watch by night, on Bethlehem Heights.

The Three Purses

By William S. Walsh (Adapted)

A LEGEND

When Saint Nicholas was Bishop of Myra, there were among his people three beautiful maidens, daughters of a nobleman. Their father was so poor that he could not afford to give them dowries, and as in that land no maid might marry without a dowry, so these three maidens could not wed the youths who loved them.

At last the father became so very poor that he no longer had money with which to buy food or clothes for his daughters, and he was overcome by shame and sorrow. As for the daughters they wept continually, for they were both cold and hungry.

One day Saint Nicholas heard of the sad state of this noble family. So at night, when the maidens were asleep, and the father was watching, sorrowful and lonely, the good saint took a handful of gold, and, tying it in a purse, set off for the nobleman's house. Creeping to the open window he threw the purse into the chamber, so that it fell on the bed of the sleeping maidens.

The father picked up the purse, and when he opened it and saw the gold, he rejoiced greatly, and awakened his daughters. He gave most of the gold to his eldest child for a dowry, and thus she was enabled to wed the young man whom she loved.

A few days later Saint Nicholas filled another purse with gold, and, as before, went by night to the nobleman's house, and tossed the purse through the open window. Thus the second daughter was enabled to marry the young man whom she loved.

Now, the nobleman felt very grateful to the unknown one who threw purses of gold into his room and he longed to know who his benefactor was and to thank him. So the next night he watched beneath the open window. And when all was dark, lo! good Saint Nicholas came for the third time, carrying a silken purse filled with gold, and as he was about to throw it on the youngest maiden's bed, the nobleman caught him by his robe, crying:—

“Ohs good Saint Nicholas! why do you hide yourself thus?”

And he kissed the saint's hands and feet, but Saint Nicholas, overcome with confusion at having his good deed discovered, begged the nobleman to tell no man what had happened.

Thus the nobleman's third daughter was enabled to marry the young man whom she loved; and she and her father and her two sisters lived happily for the remainder of their lives.

CHRISTMAS AT RED BUTTE

By Lucy Maud Montgomery

"Of course Santa Claus will come," said Jimmy Martin confidently. Jimmy was ten, and at ten it is easy to be confident. "Why, he's *got* to come because it is Christmas Eve, and he always *has* come. You know that, twins."

Yes, the twins knew it and, cheered by Jimmy's superior wisdom, their doubts passed away. There had been one terrible moment when Theodora had sighed and told them they mustn't be too much disappointed if Santa Claus did not come this year because the crops had been poor, and he mightn't have had enough presents to go around.

"That doesn't make any difference to Santa Claus," scoffed Jimmy. "You know as well as I do, Theodora Prentice, that Santa Claus is rich whether the crops fail or not. They failed three years ago, before Father died, but Santa Claus came all the same. Prob'bly you don't remember it, twins, 'cause you were too little, but I do. Of course he'll come, so don't you worry a mite. And he'll bring my skates and your dolls. He knows we're expecting them, Theodora, 'cause we wrote him a letter last week, and threw it up the chimney. And there'll be candy and nuts, of course, and Mother's gone to town to buy a turkey. I tell you we're going to have a ripping Christmas."

"Well, don't use such slangy words about it, Jimmy-boy," sighed Theodora. She couldn't bear to dampen their hopes any further, and perhaps Aunt Elizabeth might manage it if the colt sold well. But Theodora had her painful doubts, and she sighed again as she looked out of the window far down the trail that wound across the prairie, red-lighted by the declining sun of the short wintry afternoon.

"Do people always sigh like that when they get to be sixteen?" asked Jimmy curiously. "You didn't sigh like that when you were only fifteen, Theodora. I wish you wouldn't. It makes me feel funny—and it's not a nice kind of funniness either."

"It's a bad habit I've got into lately," said Theodora, trying to laugh. "Old folks are dull sometimes, you know, Jimmy-boy."

"Sixteen *is* awful old, isn't it?" said Jimmy reflectively. "I'll tell you what *I'm* going to do when I'm sixteen, Theodora. I'm going to pay off the mortgage, and buy mother a silk dress, and a piano for the twins. Won't that be elegant? I'll be able to do that 'cause I'm a man. Of course if I was only a girl I couldn't."

"I hope you'll be a good kind brave man and a real help to your mother," said Theodora softly, sitting down before the cosy fire and lifting the fat little twins into her lap.

"Oh, I'll be good to her, never you fear," assured Jimmy, squatting comfortably down on the little fur rug before the stove—the skin of the coyote his father had killed four years ago. "I believe in being good to your mother when you've only got the one. Now tell us a story, Theodora—a real jolly story, you know, with lots of fighting in it. Only please don't kill anybody. I like to hear about fighting, but I like to have all the people come out alive."

Theodora laughed, and began a story about the Riel Rebellion of '85—a story which had the double merit of being true and exciting at the same time. It was quite dark when she finished, and the twins were nodding, but Jimmy's eyes were wide open and sparkling.

"That was great," he said, drawing a long breath. "Tell us another."

"No, it's bedtime for you all," said Theodora firmly. "One story at a time is my rule, you know."

"But I want to sit up till Mother comes home," objected Jimmy.

"You can't. She may be very late, for she would have to wait to see Mr. Porter. Besides, you don't know what time Santa Claus might come—if he comes at all. If he were to drive along and see you children up instead of being sound asleep in bed, he might go right on and never call at all."

This argument was too much for Jimmy.

"All right, we'll go. But we have to hang up our stockings first. Twins, get yours."

The twins toddled off in great excitement, and brought back their Sunday stockings, which Jimmy proceeded to hang along the edge of the mantel shelf. This done, they all trooped obediently off to bed. Theodora gave another sigh, and seated herself at the window, where she could watch the moonlit prairie for Mrs. Martin's homecoming and knit at the same time.

I am afraid that you will think from all the sighing Theodora was doing that she was a very melancholy and despondent young lady. You couldn't think anything more unlike the real Theodora. She was the jolliest, bravest girl of sixteen in all Saskatchewan, as her shining brown eyes and rosy, dimpled cheeks would have told you; and her sighs were not on her own account, but simply for fear the children were going to be disappointed. She knew that they would be almost heartbroken if Santa Claus did not come, and that this would hurt the patient hardworking little mother more than all else.

Five years before this, Theodora had come to live with Uncle George and Aunt Elizabeth in the little log house at Red Butte. Her own mother had just died, and Theodora had only her big brother Donald left, and Donald had Klondike fever. The Martins were poor, but they had gladly made room for their little niece, and Theodora had lived there ever since, her aunt's right-hand girl and the beloved playmate of the children. They had been very happy until Uncle George's death two years before this Christmas Eve; but since then there had been hard times in the little log house, and though Mrs. Martin and Theodora did their best, it was a woefully hard task to make both ends meet, especially this year when their crops had been poor. Theodora and her aunt had made every sacrifice possible for the children's sake, and at least Jimmy and the twins had not felt the pinch very severely yet.

At seven Mrs. Martins bells jingled at the door and Theodora flew out. "Go right in and get warm, Auntie," she said briskly. "I'll take Ned away and unharness him."

"It's a bitterly cold night," said Mrs. Martin wearily. There was a note of discouragement in her voice that struck dismay to Theodora's heart.

"I'm afraid it means no Christmas for the children tomorrow," she thought sadly, as she led Ned away to the stable. When she returned to the kitchen Mrs. Martin was sitting by the fire, her face in her chilled hand, sobbing convulsively.

"Auntie—oh, Auntie, don't!" exclaimed Theodora impulsively. It was such a rare thing to see her plucky, resolute little aunt in tears. "You're cold and tired—I'll have a nice cup of tea for you in a trice."

"No, it isn't that," said Mrs. Martin brokenly "It was seeing those stockings hanging there. Theodora, I couldn't get a thing for the children—not a single thing. Mr. Porter would only give forty dollars for the colt, and when all the bills were paid there was barely enough left for such necessaries as we must have. I suppose I ought to feel thankful I could get those. But the thought of the children's disappointment tomorrow is more than I can bear. It would have been better to have told them long ago, but I kept building on getting more for the colt. Well, it's weak and foolish to give way like this.

We'd better both take a cup of tea and go to bed. It will save fuel."

When Theodora went up to her little room her face was very thoughtful. She took a small box from her table and carried it to the window. In it was a very pretty little gold locket hung on a narrow blue ribbon. Theodora held it tenderly in her fingers, and looked out over the moonlit prairie with a very sober face. Could she give up her dear locket—the locket Donald had given her just before he started for the Klondike? She had never thought she could do such a thing. It was almost the only thing she had to remind her of Donald—handsome, merry, impulsive, warmhearted Donald, who had gone away four years ago with a smile on his bonny face and splendid hope in his heart.

"Here's a locket for you, Gift o' God," he had said gaily—he had such a dear loving habit of calling her by the beautiful meaning of her name. A lump came into Theodora's throat as she remembered it. "I couldn't afford a chain too, but when I come back I'll bring you a rope of Klondike nuggets for it."

Then he had gone away. For two years letters had come from him regularly. Then he wrote that he had joined a prospecting party to a remote wilderness. After that was silence, deepening into anguish of suspense that finally ended in hopelessness. A rumour came that Donald Prentice was dead. None had returned from the expedition he had joined. Theodora had long ago given up all hope of ever seeing Donald again. Hence her locket was doubly dear to her.

But Aunt Elizabeth had always been so good and loving and kind to her. Could she not make the sacrifice for her sake? Yes, she could and would. Theodora flung up her head with a gesture that meant decision. She took out of the locket the bits of hair—her mother's and Donald's—which it contained (perhaps a tear or two fell as she did so) and then hastily donned her warmest cap and wraps. It was only three miles to Spencer; she could easily walk it in an hour and, as it was Christmas Eve, the shops would be open late. She muse walk, for Ned could not be taken out again, and the mare's foot was sore. Besides, Aunt Elizabeth must not know until it was done.

As stealthily as if she were bound on some nefarious errand, Theodora slipped downstairs and out of the house. The next minute she was hurrying along the trail in the moonlight. The great dazzling prairie was around her, the mystery and splendour of the northern night all about her. It was very calm and cold, but Theodora walked so briskly that she kept warm. The trail from Red Butte to Spencer was a lonely one. Mr. Lurgan's house, halfway to town, was the only dwelling on it.

When Theodora reached Spencer she made her way at once to the only jewellery store the little town contained. Mr. Benson, its owner, had been a friend of her uncle's, and Theodora felt sure that he would buy her locket. Nevertheless her heart beat quickly, and her breath came and went uncomfortably fast as she went in. Suppose he wouldn't buy it. Then there would be no Christmas for the children at Red Butte.

"Good evening, Miss Theodora," said Mr. Benson briskly. "What can I do for you?"

"I'm afraid I'm not a very welcome sort of customer, Mr. Benson," said Theodora, with an uncertain smile. "I want to sell, not buy. Could you—will you buy this locket?"

Mr. Benson pursed up his lips, took up the locket, and examined it. "Well, I don't often buy second-hand stuff," he said, after some reflection, "but I don't mind obliging you, Miss Theodora. I'll give you four dollars for this trinket."

Theodora knew the locket had cost a great deal more than that, but four dollars would get what she wanted, and she dared not ask for more. In a few minutes the locket was in Mr. Benson's possession, and Theodora, with four crisp new bills in her purse, was hurrying to the toy store. Half an hour later she was on her way back to Red Butte, with as many parcels as she could carry—Jimmy's skates, two lovely dolls for the twins, packages of nuts and candy, and a nice plump turkey. Theodora beguiled her lonely tramp by picturing the children's joy in the morning.

About a quarter of a mile past Mr. Lurgan's house the trail curved suddenly about a bluff of poplars. As Theodora rounded the turn she halted in amazement. Almost at her feet the body of a man was lying across the road. He was clad in a big fur coat, and had a fur cap pulled well down over his forehead and ears. Almost all of him that could be seen was a full bushy beard. Theodora had no idea who he was, or where he had come from. But she realized that he was unconscious, and that he would speedily freeze to death if help were not brought. The footprints of a horse galloping across the prairie suggested a fall and a runaway, but Theodora did not waste time in speculation. She ran back at full speed to Mr. Lurgan's, and roused the household. In a few minutes Mr. Lurgan and his son had hitched a horse to a wood-sleigh, and hurried down the trail to the unfortunate man.

Theodora, knowing that her assistance was not needed, and that she ought to get home as quickly as possible, went on her way as soon as she had seen the stranger in safe keeping. When she reached the little log house she crept in, cautiously put the children's gifts in their stockings, placed the turkey on the table where Aunt Elizabeth would see it the first thing in the morning, and then slipped off to bed, a very weary but very happy girl.

The joy that reigned in the little log house the next day more than repaid Theodora for her sacrifice.

"Whoopee, didn't I tell you that Santa Claus would come all right!" shouted the delighted Jimmy. "Oh, what splendid skates!"

The twins hugged their dolls in silent rapture, but Aunt Elizabeth's face was the best of all.

Then the dinner had to be prepared, and everybody had a hand in that. Just as Theodora, after a grave peep into the oven, had announced that the turkey was done, a sleigh dashed around the house. Theodora flew to answer the knock at the door, and there stood Mr. Lurgan and a big, bewhiskered, fur-coated fellow whom Theodora recognized as the stranger she had found on the trail. But—*was* he a stranger? There was something oddly familiar in those merry brown eyes. Theodora felt herself growing dizzy.

"Donald!" she gasped. "Oh, Donald!"

And then she was in the big fellow's arms, laughing and crying at the same time.

Donald it was indeed. And then followed half an hour during which everybody talked at once, and the turkey would have been burned to a crisp had it not been for the presence of mind of Mr. Lurgan who, being the least excited of them all, took it out of the oven, and set it on the back of the stove.

"To think that it was you last night, and that I never dreamed it," exclaimed Theodora. "Oh, Donald, if I hadn't gone to town!"

"I'd have frozen to death, I'm afraid," said Donald soberly. "I got into Spencer on the last train last night. I felt that I must come right out—I couldn't wait till morning. But there wasn't a team to be got for love or money—it was Christmas Eve and all the livery rigs were out. So I came on horseback. Just by that bluff something frightened my horse, and he shied violently. I was half asleep and thinking of my little sister, and I went off like a shot. I suppose I struck my head against a tree. Anyway, I knew nothing more until I came to in Mr. Lurgan's kitchen. I wasn't much hurt—feel none the worse of it except for a sore head and shoulder. But, oh, Gift o' God, how you have grown! I can't realize that you are the little sister I left four years ago. I suppose you have been thinking I was dead?"

"Yes, and, oh, Donald, where *have* you been?"

"Well, I went way up north with a prospecting party. We had a tough time the first year, I can tell you, and some of us never came back. We weren't in a country where post offices were lying round loose either, you see. Then at last, just as we were about giving up in despair, we struck it rich. I've brought a snug little pile home with me, and things are going to look up in this log house, Gift o' God. There'll be no more worrying for you dear people over mortgages."

"I'm so glad—for Auntie's sake," said Theodora, with shining eyes. "But, oh, Donald, it's best of all just to have you back. I'm so perfectly happy that I don't know what to do or say."

"Well, I think you might have dinner," said Jimmy in an injured tone. "The turkey's getting stone cold, and I'm most starving. I just can't stand it another minute."

So, with a laugh, they all sat down to the table and ate the merriest Christmas dinner the little log house had ever known.

A Christmas Matinee

M.A.L. Lane

It was the day before Christmas in the year 189-. Snow was falling heavily in the streets of Boston, but the crowd of shoppers seemed undiminished. As the storm increased, groups gathered at the corners and in sheltering doorways to wait for belated cars; but the holiday cheer was in the air, and there was no grumbling. Mothers dragging tired children through the slush of the streets; pretty girls hurrying home for the holidays; here and there a harassed-looking man with perhaps a single package which he had taken a whole morning to select—all had the same spirit of tolerant good-humor.

"School Street! School Street!" called the conductor of an electric car. A group of young people at the farther end of the car started to their feet. One of them, a young man wearing a heavy fur-trimmed coat, addressed the conductor angrily.

"I said, 'Music Hall,' didn't I?" he demanded. "Now we've got to walk back in the snow because of your stupidity!"

"Oh, never mind, Frank!" one of the girls interposed. "We ought to have been looking out ourselves! Six of us, and we went by without a thought! It is all Mrs. Tirrell's fault! She shouldn't have been so entertaining!"

The young matron dimpled and blushed. "That's charming of you, Maidie," she said, gathering up her silk skirts as she prepared to step down into the pond before her. "The compliment makes up for the blame. But how it snows!"

"It doesn't matter. We all have gaiters on," returned Maidie Williams, undisturbed.

"Fares, please!" said the conductor stolidly.

Frank Armstrong thrust his gloved hand deep into his pocket with angry vehemence. "There's your money," he said, "and be quick about the change, will you? We've lost time enough!"

The man counted out the change with stiff, red fingers, closed his lips firmly as if to keep back an obvious rejoinder, rang up the six fares with careful accuracy, and gave the signal to go ahead. The car went on into the drifting storm.

Armstrong laughed shortly as he rapidly counted the bits of silver lying in his open palm. He turned instinctively, but two or three cars were already between him and the one he was looking for.

"The fellow must be an imbecile," he said, rejoining the group on the crossing. "He's given me back a dollar and twenty cents, and I handed him a dollar bill."

"Oh, can't you stop him?" cried Maidie Williams, with a backward step into the wet street.

The Harvard junior, who was carrying her umbrella, protested: "What's the use. Miss Williams? He'll make it up before he gets to Scollay Square, you may be sure. Those chaps don't lose anything. Why, the other day, I gave one a quarter and he went off as cool as you please. 'Where's my change?' said I. 'You gave me a nickel,' said he. And there wasn't anybody to swear that I didn't except myself, and I didn't count."

"But that doesn't make any difference," insisted the girl warmly. "Because one conductor was dishonest, we needn't be. I beg your pardon, Frank, but it does seem to me just stealing."

"Oh, come along!" said her cousin, with an easy laugh. "I guess the West End Corporation won't go without their dinners to-morrow. Here, Maidie, here's the ill-gotten fifty cents. *I* think you ought to treat us all after the concert; still, I won't urge you. I wash my hands of all responsibility. But I do wish you hadn't such an unpleasant conscience."

Maidie flushed under the sting of his cousinly rudeness, but she went on quietly with the rest. It was evident that any attempt to overtake the car was out of the question.

"Did you notice his number, Frank?" she asked, suddenly.

"No, I never thought of it" said Frank, stopping short. "However, I probably shouldn't make any complaint if I had. I shall forget all about it tomorrow. I find it's never safe to let the sun go down on my wrath. It's very likely not to be there the next day."

"I wasn't thinking of making a complaint," said Maidie; but the two young men were enjoying the small joke too much to notice what she said.

The great doorway of Music Hall was just ahead. In a moment the party were within its friendly shelter, stamping off the snow. The girls were adjusting veils and hats with adroit feminine touches; the pretty chaperon was beaming approval upon them, and the young men were taking off their wet overcoats, when Maidie turned again in sudden desperation.

"Mr. Harris," she said, rather faintly, for she did not like to make herself disagreeable, "do you suppose that car comes right back from Scollay Square?"

"What car?" asked Walter Harris, blankly. "Oh, the one we came in? Yes, I suppose it does. They're running all the time, anyway. Why, you are not sick, are you, Miss Williams?"

There was genuine concern in his tone. This girl, with her sweet, vibrant voice, her clear gray eyes, seemed very charming to him. She wasn't beautiful, perhaps, but she was the kind of girl he liked. There was a steady earnestness in the gray eyes that made him think of his mother.

"No," said Maidie, slowly. "I'm all right, thank you. But I wish I could find that man again. I know sometimes they have to make it up if their accounts are wrong, and I couldn't—we couldn't feel very comfortable—"

Frank Armstrong interrupted her. "Maidie," he said, with the studied calmness with which one speaks to an unreasonable child, "you are perfectly absurd. Here it is within five minutes of the tune for the concert to begin. It is impossible to tell when that car is coming back. You are making us all very uncomfortable. Mrs. Tirrell, won't you please tell her not to spoil our afternoon?"

"I think he's right, Maidie," said Mrs. Tirrell. "It's very nice of you to feel so sorry for the poor man, but he really was very careless. It was all his own fault. And just think how far he made us walk! My feet are quite damp. We ought to go in directly or we shall all take cold, and I'm sure you wouldn't like that, my dear."

She led the way as she spoke, the two girls and young Armstrong following. Maidie hesitated. It was so easy to go in, to forget everything in the light and warmth and excitement.

"No," said she, very firmly, and as much to herself as to the young man who stood waiting for her. "I must go back and try to make it right. I'm so sorry, Mr. Harris, but if you will tell them—"

"Why, I'm going with you, of course" said the young fellow, impulsively. "If I'd only looked once at the man I'd go alone, but I shouldn't know him from Adam."

Maidie laughed. "Oh, I don't want to lose the whole concert, Mr. Harris, and Frank, has all the tickets. You must go after them and try to make my peace. I'll come just as soon as I can. Don't wait for me, please. If you'll come and look for me here the first number, and not let them scold me too much—" She ended with an imploring little catch in her breath that was almost a sob.

"They sha'n't say a word, Miss Williams!" cried Walter Harris, with honest admiration in his eyes.

But she was gone already, and conscious that further delay was only making matters worse, he went on into the hall.

Meanwhile, the car swung heavily along the wet rails on its way to the turning-point. It was nearly empty now. An old gentleman and his nurse were the only occupants. Jim Stevens, the conductor, had stepped inside the car.

"Too bad I forgot those young people wanted to get off at Music Hall," he was thinking to himself. "I don't see how I came to do it. That chap looked as if he wanted to complain of me, and I don't know as I blame him. I'd have said I was sorry if he hadn't been so sharp with his tongue. I hope he won't complain just now. 'Twould be a pretty bad time for me to get into trouble, with Mary and the baby both sick. I'm too sleepy to be good for much, that's a fact. Sitting up three nights running takes hold of a fellow somehow when he's at work all day. The rent's paid, that's one thing, if it hasn't left me but half a dollar to my name. Hullo!" He was struck by a sudden distinct recollection of the coins he had returned. "Why, I gave him fifty cents too much!"

He glanced up at the dial which indicated the fares and began to count the change in his pocket. He knew exactly how much money he had had at the beginning of the trip. He counted carefully. Then he plunged his hand into the heavy canvas pocket of his coat. Perhaps he had half a dollar there. No, it was empty!

He faced the fact reluctantly. Fifty cents short, ten fares! Gone into the pocket of the young gentleman with the fur collar! The conductor's hand shook as he put the money back in his pocket. It meant—what did it mean? He drew a long breath.

Christmas Eve! A dark dreary little room upstairs in a noisy tenement house. A pale, thin woman on a shabby lounge vainly trying to quiet a fretful child. The child is thin and pale, too, with a hard, racking cough. There is a small fire in the stove, a very small fire; coal is so high. The medicine stands on the shelf. "Medicine won't do much good," the doctor had said;"he needs beef and cream."

Jim's heart sank at the thought. He could almost hear the baby asking;"Isn't papa coming soon? Isn't he, mamma?"

"Poor little kid!" Jim said, softly, under his breath. "And I shan't have a thing to take home to him; nor Mary's violets, either. It'll be the first Christmas that ever happened. I suppose that chap would think it was ridiculous for me to be buying violets. He wouldn't understand what the flowers mean to Mary. Perhaps he didn't notice I gave him too much. That kind don't know how much they have. They just pull it out as if it was newspaper."

The conductor went out into the snow to help the nurse, who was assisting the old gentleman to the ground. Then the car swung on again. Jim turned up the collar of his coat about his ears and stamped his feet. There was the florist's shop where he had meant to buy the violets, and the toy-shop was just around the corner.

A thought flashed across his tired brain. "Plenty of men would do it; they do it every day. Nobody ever would be the poorer for it. This car will be crowded going home. I needn't ring in every fare; nobody could tell. But Mary! She wouldn't touch those violets if she knew. And she'd know. I'd have to tell her. I couldn't keep it from her, she's that quick."

He jumped off to adjust the trolley with a curious sense of unreality. It couldn't be that he was really going home this Christmas Eve with empty hands. Well, they must all suffer together for his carelessness. It was his own fault, but it was hard. And he was so tired!

To his amazement he found his eyes were blurred as he watched the people crowding into the car. What? Was he going to cry like a baby—he, a great burly man of thirty years?

"It's no use," he thought. "I couldn't do it. The first time I gave Mary violets was the night she said she'd marry me. I told her then I'd do my best to make her proud of me. I guess she wouldn't be very proud of a man who could cheat. She'd rather starve than have a ribbon she couldn't pay for."

He rang up a dozen fares with a steady hand. The temptation was over. Six more strokes—then nine without a falter. He even imagined the bell rang more distinctly than usual, even encouragingly. The car stopped. Jim flung the door open with a triumphant sweep of his arm. He felt ready to face the world. But the baby—his arm dropped. It was hard.

He turned to help the young girl who was waiting at the step. Through the whirling snow he saw her eager face, with a quick recognition lighting the steady eyes, and wondered dimly, as he stood with his hand on the signal-strap, where he could have seen her before.

He knew immediately.

"There was a mistake," she said, with a shy tremor in her voice. "You gave us too much change and here it is." She held out to Jim the piece of silver which had given him such an unhappy quarter of an hour.

He took it like one dazed. Would the young lady think he was crazy to care so much about so small a coin? He must say something. "Thank you, miss," he stammered as well as he could. "You see, I thought it was gone—and there's the baby—and it's Christmas Eve—and my wife's sick—and you can't understand—"

It certainly was not remarkable that she couldn't.

"But I do," she said, simply. "I was afraid of that. And I thought perhaps there was a baby, so I brought my Christmas present for her," and something else dropped into Jim's cold hand.

"What you waiting for?" shouted the motorman from the front platform. The girl had disappeared in the snow.

Jim rang the bell to go ahead, and gazed again at the two shining half dollars in his hand.

"I didn't have a chance to tell her," he explained to his wife late in the evening, as he sat in a tiny rocking-chair several sizes too small for him, "that the baby wasn't a her at all, though if I thought he'd grow up into such a lovely one as she is, I don't know but I almost wish he was."

"Poor Jim!" said Mary, with a little laugh as she put up her hand to stroke his rough cheek. "I guess you're tired."

"And I should say," he added, stretching out his long legs toward the few red sparks in the bottom of the grate, "I should say she had tears in her eyes, too, but I was that near crying myself I couldn't be sure."

The little room was sweet with the odour of English violets. Asleep in the bed lay the boy, a toy horse clasped close to his breast.

"Bless her heart!" said Mary, softly.

"Well, Miss Williams," said Walter Harris, as he sprang to meet a snow-covered figure coming swiftly along the sidewalk. "I can see that you found him. You've lost the first number, but they won't scold you—not this time."

The girl turned a radiant face upon him. "Thank you," she said, shaking the snowy crystals from her skirt. "I don't care now if they do. I should have lost more than that if I had stayed."

THE LITTLE MATCH GIRL

By Hans Christian Anderson

Most terribly cold it was; it snowed, and was nearly quite dark, and evening—the last evening of the year. In this cold and darkness there went along the street a poor little girl, bareheaded, and with naked feet. When she left home she had slippers on, it is true; but what was the good of that? They were very large slippers, which her mother had hitherto worn; so large were they; and the poor little thing lost them as she scuffled away across the street, because of two carriages that rolled by dreadfully fast.

One slipper was nowhere to be found; the other had been laid hold of by an urchin, and off he ran with it; he thought it would do capitally for a cradle when he some day or other should have children himself. So the little maiden walked on with her tiny naked feet, that were quite red and blue from cold. She carried a quantity of matches in an old apron, and she held a bundle of them in her hand. Nobody had bought anything of her the whole livelong day; no one had given her a single farthing.

She crept along trembling with cold and hunger—a very picture of sorrow, the poor little thing!

The flakes of snow covered her long fair hair, which fell in beautiful curls around her neck; but of that, of course, she never once now thought. From all the windows the candles were gleaming, and it smelt so deliciously of roast goose, for you know it was New Year's Eve; yes, of that she thought.

In a corner formed by two houses, of which one advanced more than the other, she seated herself down and cowered together. Her little feet she had drawn close up to her, but she grew colder and colder, and to go home she did not venture, for she had not sold any matches and could not bring a farthing of money: from her father she would certainly get blows, and at home it was cold too, for above her she had only the roof, through which the wind whistled, even though the largest cracks were stopped up with straw and rags.

Her little hands were almost numbed with cold. Oh! a match might afford her a world of comfort, if she only dared take a single one out of the bundle, draw it against the wall, and warm her fingers by it. She drew one out. "Rischt!" how it blazed, how it burnt! It was a warm, bright flame, like a candle, as she held her hands over it: it was a wonderful light. It seemed really to the little maiden as though she were sitting before a large iron stove, with burnished brass feet and a brass ornament at top. The fire burned with such blessed influence; it warmed so delightfully. The little girl had already stretched out her feet to warm them too; but—the small flame went out, the stove vanished: she had only the remains of the burnt-out match in her hand.

She rubbed another against the wall: it burned brightly, and where the light fell on the wall, there the wall became transparent like a veil, so that she could see into the room. On the table was spread a snow-white tablecloth; upon it was a splendid porcelain service, and the roast goose was steaming famously with its stuffing of apple and dried plums. And what was still more capital to behold was, the goose hopped down from the dish, reeled about on the floor with knife and fork in its breast, till it came up to the poor little girl; when—the match went out and nothing but the thick, cold, damp wall was left behind. She lighted another match. Now there she was sitting under the most magnificent Christmas tree: it was still larger, and more decorated than the one which she had seen through the glass door in the rich merchant's house.

Thousands of lights were burning on the green branches, and gaily-colored pictures, such as she had seen in the shop-windows, looked down upon her. The little maiden stretched out her hands towards them when—the match went out. The lights of the Christmas tree rose higher and higher, she saw them now as stars in heaven; one fell down and formed a long trail of fire.

"Someone is just dead!" said the little girl; for her old grandmother, the only person who had loved her, and who was now no more, had told her, that when a star falls, a soul ascends to God.

She drew another match against the wall: it was again light, and in the lustre there stood the old grandmother, so bright and radiant, so mild, and with such an expression of love.

"Grandmother!" cried the little one. "Oh, take me with you! You go away when the match burns out; you vanish like the warm stove, like the delicious roast goose, and like the magnificent Christmas tree!" And she rubbed the whole bundle of matches quickly against the wall, for she wanted to be quite sure of keeping her grandmother near her. And the matches gave such a brilliant light that it was brighter than at noon-day: never formerly had the grandmother been so beautiful and so tall. She took the little maiden, on her arm, and both flew in brightness and in joy so high, so very high, and then above was neither cold, nor hunger, nor anxiety—they were with God.

But in the corner, at the cold hour of dawn, sat the poor girl, with rosy cheeks and with a smiling mouth, leaning against the wall—frozen to death on the last evening of the old year. Stiff and stark sat the child there with her matches, of which one bundle had been burnt. "She wanted to warm herself," people said. No one had the slightest suspicion of what beautiful things she had seen; no one even dreamed of the splendor in which, with her grandmother she had entered on the joys of a new year.

A STORY OF THE CHRIST-CHILD

By Elizabeth Harrison

Once upon a time, a long, long time ago, on the night before Christmas, a little child was wandering all alone through the streets of a great city. There were many people on the street, fathers and mothers, sisters and brothers, uncles and aunts, and even gray-haired grandfathers and grandmothers, all of whom were hurrying home with bundles of presents for each other and for their little ones. Fine carriages rolled by, express wagons rattled past, even old carts were pressed into service, and all things seemed in a hurry and glad with expectation of the coming Christmas morning.

From some of the windows bright lights were already beginning to stream until it was almost as bright as day. But the little child seemed to have no home, and wandered about listlessly from street to street. No one took any notice of him except perhaps Jack Frost, who bit his bare toes and made the ends of his fingers tingle. The north wind, too, seemed to notice the child, for it blew against him and pierced his ragged garments through and through, causing him to shiver with cold. Home after home he passed, looking with longing eyes through the windows, in upon the glad, happy children, most of whom were helping to trim the Christmas trees for the coming morrow.

"Surely," said the child to himself, "where there is so must gladness and happiness, some of it may be for me." So with timid steps he approached a large and handsome house. Through the windows, he could see a tall and stately Christmas tree already lighted. Many presents hung upon it. Its green boughs were trimmed with gold and silver ornaments. Slowly he climbed up the broad steps and gently rapped at the door. It was opened by a large man-servant. He had a kindly face, although his voice was deep and gruff. He looked at the little child for a moment, then sadly shook his head and said, "Go down off the steps. There is no room here for such as you." He looked sorry as he spoke; possibly he remembered his own little ones at home, and was glad that they were not out in this cold and bitter night. Through the open door a bright light shone, and the warm air, filled with fragrance of the Christmas pine, rushed out from the inner room and greeted the little wanderer with a kiss. As the child turned back into the cold and darkness, he wondered why the footman had spoken thus, for surely, thought he, those little children would love to have another companion join them in their joyous Christmas festival. But the little children inside did not even know that he had knocked at the door.

The street grew colder and darker as the child passed on. He went sadly forward, saying to himself, "Is there no one in all this great city who will share the

Christmas with me?" Farther and farther down the street he wandered, to where the homes were not so large and beautiful. There seemed to be little children inside of nearly all the houses. They were dancing and frolicking about. Christmas trees could be seen in nearly every window, with beautiful dolls and trumpets and picture-books and balls and tops and other dainty toys hung upon them. In one window the child noticed a little lamb made of soft white wool. Around its neck was tied a red ribbon. It had evidently been hung on the tree for one of the children. The little stranger stopped before this window and looked long and earnestly at the beautiful things inside, but most of all was he drawn toward the white lamb. At last creeping up to the window-pane, he gently tapped upon it. A little girl came to the window and looked out into the dark street where the snow had now begun to fall. She saw the child, but she only frowned and shook her head and said, "Go away and come some other time. We are too busy to take care of you now." Back into the dark, cold streets he turned again. The wind was whirling past him and seemed to say, "Hurry on, hurry on, we have no time to stop. 'Tis Christmas Eve and everybody is in a hurry to-night."

Again and again the little child rapped softly at door or window-pane. At each place he was refused admission. One mother feared he might have some ugly disease which her darlings would catch; another father said he had only enough for his own children and none to spare for beggars. Still another told him to go home where he belonged, and not to trouble other folks.

The hours passed; later grew the night, and colder grew the wind, and darker seemed the street. Farther and farther the little one wandered. There was scarcely any one left upon the street by this time, and the few who remained did not seem to see the child, when suddenly ahead of him there appeared a bright, single ray of light. It shone through the darkness into the child's eyes. He looked up smilingly and said, "I will go where the small light beckons, perhaps they will share their Christmas with me."

Hurrying past all the other houses, he soon reached the end of the street and went straight up to the window from which the light was streaming. It was a poor, little, low house, but the child cared not for that. The light seemed still to call him in. From what do you suppose the light came? Nothing but a tallow candle which had been placed in an old cup with a broken handle, in the window, as a glad token of Christmas Eve. There was neither curtain nor shade to the small, square window and as the little child looked in he saw standing upon a neat wooden table a branch of a Christmas tree. The room was plainly furnished but it was very clean. Near the fireplace sat a lovely faced mother with a little two-year-old on her knee and an older child beside her. The two children were looking into their mother's face and listening to a story. She must have been telling them a Christmas story, I think.

A few bright coals were burning in the fireplace, and all seemed light and warm within.

The little wanderer crept closer and closer to the window-pane. So sweet was the mother's face, so loving seemed the little children, that at last he took courage and tapped gently, very gently on the door. The mother stopped talking, the little children looked up. "What was that, mother?" asked the little girl at her side. "I think it was some one tapping on the door," replied the mother. "Run as quickly as you can and open it, dear, for it is a bitter cold night to keep any one waiting in this storm." "Oh, mother, I think it was the bough of the tree tapping against the window-pane," said the little girl. "Do please go on with our story." Again the little wanderer tapped upon the door. "My child, my child," exclaimed the mother, rising, "that certainly was a rap on the door. Run quickly and open it. No one must be left out in the cold on our beautiful Christmas Eve."

The child ran to the door and threw it wide open. The mother saw the ragged stranger standing without, cold and shivering, with bare head and almost bare feet. She held out both hands and drew him into the warm, bright room. "You poor, dear child," was all she said, and putting her arms around him, she drew him close to her breast. "He is very cold, my children," she exclaimed. "We must warm him." "And," added the little girl, "we must love him and give him some of our Christmas, too." "Yes," said the mother, "but first let us warm him—"

The mother sat down by the fire with the little child on her lap, and her own little ones warmed his half-frozen hands in theirs. The mother smoothed his tangled curls, and, bending low over his head, kissed the child's face. She gathered the three little ones in her arms and the candle and the fire light shone over them. For a moment the room was very still. By and by the little girl said softly, to her mother, "May we not light the Christmas tree, and let him see how beautiful it looks?" "Yes," said the mother. With that she seated the child on a low stool beside the fire, and went herself to fetch the few simple ornaments which from year to year she had saved for her children's Christmas tree. They were soon so busy that they did not notice the room had filled with a strange and brilliant light. They turned and looked at the spot where the little wanderer sat. His ragged clothes had changed to garments white and beautiful; his tangled curls seemed like a halo of golden light about his head; but most glorious of all was his face, which shone with a light so dazzling that they could scarcely look upon it.

In silent wonder they gazed at the child. Their little room seemed to grow larger and larger, until it was as wide as the whole world, the roof of their low house seemed to expand and rise, until it reached to the sky.

With a sweet and gentle smile the wonderful child looked upon them for a moment, and then slowly rose and floated through the air, above the treetops, beyond the church spire, higher even than the clouds themselves, until he appeared to them to be a shining star in the sky above. At last he disappeared from sight. The astonished children turned in hushed awe to their mother, and said in a whisper, "Oh, mother, it was the Christ-Child, was it not?" And the mother answered in a low tone, "Yes."

And it is said, dear children, that each Christmas Eve the little Christ-Child wanders through some town or village, and those who receive him and take him into their homes and hearts have given to them this marvellous vision which is denied to others.

The Steadfast Tin Soldier

By Hans Christian Anderson

There were once twenty-five tin soldiers, who were all brothers, for they were cast out of one old tin spoon. They held their muskets, and their faces were turned to the enemy; red and blue, ever so fine, were the uniforms. The first thing they heard in this world, when the cover was taken from the box where they lay, were the words, "Tin soldiers!" A little boy shouted it, and clapped his hands. He had got them because it was his birthday, and now he set them up on the table. Each soldier was just like the other, only one was a little different. He had but one leg, for he had been cast last, and there was not enough tin. But he stood on his one leg just as firm as the others on two, so he was just the one to be famous.

On the table where they were set up stood a lot of other playthings; but what caught your eye was a pretty castle of paper. Through the little windows you could see right into the halls. Little trees stood in front, around a bit of looking-glass which was meant for a lake. Wax swans swam on it and were reflected in it. That was all very pretty, but still the prettiest thing was a little girl who stood right in the castle gate. She was cut out of paper too, but she had a silk dress, and a little narrow blue ribbon across her shoulders, on which was a sparkling star as big as her whole face. The little girl lifted her arms gracefully in the air, for she was a dancer; and then she lifted one leg so high that the tin soldier could not find it at all, and thought that she had only one leg, just like himself.

"That would be the wife for me," thought he, "but she is too fine for me. She lives in a castle, and I have only a box, which I have to share with twenty-four. That is no house for her. But I will see whether I can make her acquaintance." Then he lay down at full length behind a snuff-box which was on the table. From there he could watch the trig little lady who kept standing on one leg without losing her balance. When evening came, the other tin soldiers were all put in their box, and the people in the house went to bed. Then the playthings began to play, first at "visiting," then at "war" and at "dancing." The tin soldiers rattled in their box, for they would have liked to join in it, but they could not get the cover off. The nutcracker turned somersaults, and the pencil scrawled over the slate. There was such a racket that the canary-bird woke up and began to sing, and that in verses. The only ones that did not stir were the tin soldier and the little dancer. She stood straight on tiptoe and stretched up both arms; he was just as steadfast on his one leg. He did not take his eyes from her a moment.

Now it struck twelve, and bang! up went the cover of the snuff-box, but it wasn't tobacco in it: no, but a little black Troll. It was a trick box.

"Tin soldier!" said the Troll, "will you stare your eyes out?" But the tin soldier made believe he did not hear. "You wait till morning!" said the Troll.

When morning came, and the children got up, the tin soldier was put on the window ledge; and whether it was the Troll, or a gust of wind, all at once the window flew open and the tin soldier fell head first from the third story. That was an awful fall. He stretched his leg straight up, and stuck with his bayonet and cap right between the paving-stones.

The maid and the little boy came right down to hunt for him, but they couldn't see him, though they came so near that they almost trod on him. If the tin soldier had called "Here I am," they surely would have found him; but since he was in uniform he did not think it proper to call aloud.

Now it began to rain. The drops chased one another. It was a regular shower. When that was over, two street boys came along.

"Hallo!" said one, "There's a tin soldier. He must be off and sail."

Then they made a boat out of a newspaper, put the tin soldier in it, and made him sail down the gutter. Both boys ran beside it, and clapped their hands. Preserve us! What waves there were in the gutter, and what a current! It must have rained torrents. The paper boat rocked up and down, and sometimes it whirled around so that the tin soldier shivered. But he remained steadfast, did not lose color, looked straight ahead and held his musket firm.

All at once the boat plunged under a long gutter-bridge. It was as dark there as it had been in his box.

"Where am I going now?" thought he. "Yes, yes, that is the Troll's fault. Oh! if the little lady were only in the boat, I would not care if it were twice as dark."

At that instant there came a great water-rat who lived under the gutter-bridge.

"Have you a pass?" said the rat. "Show me your pass."

But the tin soldier kept still, and only held his musket the firmer. The boat rushed on, and the rat behind. Oh! how he gnashed his teeth, and called to the sticks and straws:--

"Stop him! Stop him! He has not paid toll. He has showed no pass."

But the current got stronger and stronger. Before he got to the end of the bridge the tin soldier could see daylight, but he heard also a rushing noise that might frighten a brave man's heart. Just think! at the end of the bridge the gutter emptied into a great canal, which for him was as dangerous as for us to sail down a great waterfall.

He was so near it already that he could not stop. The boat went down. The poor tin soldier held himself as straight as he could. No one should say of him that he had ever blinked his eyes. The boat whirled three or four times and filled with water. It had to sink. The tin soldier stood up to his neck in water, and deeper, deeper sank the boat. The paper grew weaker and weaker. Now the waves went over the soldier's head. Then he thought of the pretty little dancer whom he never was to see again, and there rang in the tin soldier's ears:--

"Farewell, warrior! farewell! Death shalt thou stiffer."

Now the paper burst in two, and the tin soldier fell through,--but in that minute he was swallowed by a big fish.

Oh! wasn't it dark in there. It was worse even than under the gutter-bridge, and besides, so cramped. But the tin soldier was steadfast, and lay at full length, musket in hand.

The fish rushed around and made the most fearful jumps. At last he was quite still, and something went through him like a lightning flash. Then a bright light rushed in, and somebody called aloud, "The tin soldier!" The fish had been caught, brought to market, sold, and been taken to the kitchen, where the maid had slit it up with a big knife. She caught the soldier around the body and carried him into the parlor, where everybody wanted to see such a remarkable man who had traveled about in a fish's belly. But the tin soldier was not a bit proud. They put him on the table, and there--well! what strange things do happen in the world--the tin soldier was in the very same room that he had been in before. He saw the same children, and the same playthings were on the table, the splendid castle with the pretty little dancer; she was still standing on one leg, and had the other high in the air. She was steadfast, too. That touched the tin soldier so that he could almost have wept tin tears, but that would not have been proper. He looked at her and she looked at him, but they said nothing at all.

Suddenly one of the little boys seized the tin soldier and threw him right into the tile-stove, although he had no reason to. It was surely the Troll in the box who was to blame.

The tin soldier stood in full light and felt a fearful heat; but whether that came from the real fire, or from his glowing love, he could not tell. All the color had faded from him; but whether this had happened on the journey, or whether it came from care, no one could say. He looked at the little girl and she looked at him. He felt that he was melting, but still he stood steadfast, musket in hand. Then a door opened. A whiff of air caught the dancer, and she flew like a sylph right into the tile-stove to the tin soldier, blazed up in flame, and was gone. Then the tin soldier melted to a lump, and when the maid next day took out the ashes, she found him as a little tin heart. But of the dancer only the star was left, and that was burnt coal-black.

WHY THE CHIMES RAN

By Raymond McAlden

There was once in a faraway country where few people have ever travelled, a wonderful church. It stood on a high hill in the midst of a great city; and every Sunday, as well as on sacred days like Christmas, thousands of people climbed the hill to its great archways, looking like lines of ants all moving in the same direction.

When you came to the building itself, you found stone columns and dark passages, and a grand entrance leading to the main room of the church. This room was so long that one standing at the doorway could scarcely see to the other end, where the choir stood by the marble altar. In the farthest corner was the organ; and this organ was so loud, that sometimes when it played, the people for miles around would close their shutters and prepare for a great thunderstorm. Altogether, no such church as this was ever seen before, especially when it was lighted up for some festival, and crowded with people, young and old. But the strangest thing about the whole building was the wonderful chime of bells.

At one corner of the church was a great gray tower, with ivy growing over it as far up as one could see. I say as far as one could see, because the tower was quite great enough to fit the great church, and it rose so far into the sky that it was only in very fair weather that any one claimed to be able to see the top. Even then one could not be certain that it was in sight. Up, and up, and up climbed the stones and the ivy; and as the men who built the church had been dead for hundreds of years, every one had forgotten how high the tower was supposed to be.

Now all the people knew that at the top of the tower was a chime of Christmas bells. They had hung there ever since the church had been built, and were the most beautiful bells in the world. Some thought it was because a great musician had cast them and arranged them in their place; others said it was because of the great height, which reached up where the air was clearest and purest; however that might be no one who had ever heard the chimes denied that they were the sweetest in the world. Some described them as sounding like angels far up in the sky; others as sounding like strange winds singing through the trees.

But the fact was that no one had heard them for years and years. There was an old man living not far from the church who said that his mother had spoken of hearing them when she was a little girl, and he was the only one who was sure of as much as that. They were Christmas chimes, you see, and were not meant to be played by men or on common days. It was the custom on Christmas Eve for all the people to bring to the church their offerings to the Christ-Child; and when the greatest and best offering was laid on the altar there used to come sounding through the music of the choir the Christmas chimes far up in the tower. Some said that the wind rang them, and others, that they were so high that the angels could set them swinging. But for many long years they had never been heard. It was said that people had been growing less careful of their gifts for the Christ-Child, and that no offering was brought great enough to deserve the music of the chimes.

Every Christmas Eve the rich people still crowded to the altar, each one trying to bring some better gift than any other, without giving anything that he wanted for himself, and the church was crowded with those who thought that perhaps the wonderful bells might be heard again. But although the service was splendid, and the offerings plenty, only the roar of the wind could be heard, far up in the stone tower.

Now, a number of miles from the city, in a little country village, where nothing could be seen of the great church but glimpses of the tower when the weather was fine, lived a boy named Pedro, and his little brother. They knew very little about the Christmas chimes, but they had heard of the service in the church on Christmas Eve, and had a secret plan which they had often talked over when by themselves, to go to see the beautiful celebration.

"Nobody can guess, Little Brother," Pedro would say;"all the fine things there are to see and hear; and I have even heard it said that the Christ-Child sometimes comes down to bless the service. What if we could see Him?"

The day before Christmas was bitterly cold, with a few lonely snowflakes flying in the air, and a hard white crust on the ground. Sure enough Pedro and Little Brother were able to slip quietly away early in the afternoon; and although the walking was hard in the frosty air, before nightfall they had trudged so far, hand in hand, that they saw the lights of the big city just ahead of them. Indeed they were about to enter one of the great gates in the wall that surrounded it, when they saw something dark on the snow near their path, and stepped aside to look at it.

It was a poor woman, who had fallen just outside the city, too sick and tired to get in where she might have found shelter. The soft snow made of a drift a sort of pillow for her, and she would soon be so sound asleep, in the wintry air, that no one could ever waken her again. All this Pedro saw in a moment and he knelt down beside her and tried to rouse her, even tugging at her arm a little, as though he would have tried to carry her away. He turned her face toward him, so that he could rub some of the snow on it, and when he had looked at her silently a moment he stood up again, and said:

"It's no use, Little Brother. You will have to go on alone."

"Alone?" cried Little Brother. "And you not see the Christmas festival?"

"No," said Pedro, and he could not keep back a bit of a choking sound in his throat. "See this poor woman. Her face looks like the Madonna in the chapel window, and she will freeze to death if nobody cares for her. Every one has gone to the church now, but when you come back you can bring some one to help her. I will rub her to keep her from freezing, and perhaps get her to eat the bun that is left in my pocket."

"But I cannot bear to leave you, and go on alone," said Little Brother.

"Both of us need not miss the service," said Pedro, "and it had better be I than you. You can easily find your way to church; and you must see and hear everything twice, Little Brother—once for you and once for me. I am sure the Christ-Child must know how I should love to come with you and worship Him; and oh! if you get a chance, Little Brother, to slip up to the altar without getting in any one's way, take this little silver piece of mine, and lay it down for my offering, when no one is looking. Do not forget where you have left me, and forgive me for not going with you."

In this way he hurried Little Brother off to the city and winked hard to keep back the tears, as he heard the crunching footsteps sounding farther and farther away in the twilight. It was pretty hard to lose the music and splendour of the Christmas celebration that he had been planning for so long, and spend the time instead in that lonely place in the snow.

The great church was a wonderful place that night. Every one said that it had never looked so bright and beautiful before. When the organ played and the thousands of people sang, the walls shook with the sound, and little Pedro, away outside the city wall, felt the earth tremble around them.

At the close of the service came the procession with the offerings to be laid on the altar. Rich men and great men marched proudly up to lay down their gifts to the Christ-Child. Some brought wonderful jewels, some baskets of gold so heavy that they could scarcely carry them down the aisle. A great writer laid down a book that he had been making for years and years. And last of all walked the king of the country, hoping with all the rest to win for himself the chime of the Christmas bells. There went a great murmur through the church as the people saw the king take from his head the royal crown, all set with precious stones, and lay it gleaming on the altar, as his offering to the Holy Child. "Surely," every one said, "we shall hear the bells now, for nothing like this has ever happened before."

But still only the cold old wind was heard in the tower and the people shook their heads; and some of them said, as they had before, that they never really believed the story of the chimes, and doubted if they ever rang at all.

The procession was over, and the choir began the closing hymn. Suddenly the organist stopped playing; and every one looked at the old minister, who was standing by the altar, holding up his hand for silence. Not a sound could be heard from any one in the church, but as all the people strained their ears to listen, there came softly, but distinctly, swinging through the air, the sound of the chimes in the tower. So far away, and yet so clear the music seemed—so much sweeter were the notes than anything that had been heard before, rising and falling away up there in the sky, that the people in the church sat for a moment as still as though something held each of them by the shoulders. Then they all stood up together and stared straight at the altar, to see what great gift had awakened the long silent bells.

But all that the nearest of them saw was the childish figure of Little Brother, who had crept softly down the aisle when no one was looking, and had laid Pedro's little piece of silver on the altar.

How Christmas Came to the Santa Maria Flats

By Elia W. Peattie

There were twenty-six flat children, and none of them had ever been flat children until that year. Previously they had all been home children. and as such had, of course, had beautiful Christmases, in which their relations with Santa Claus had been of the most intimate and personal nature.

Now, owing to their residence in the Santa Maria flats, and the Lease, all was changed. The Lease was a strange forbiddance, a ukase issued by a tyrant, which took from children their natural liberties and rights.

Though, to be sure—as every one of the flat children knew—they were in the greatest kind of luck to be allowed to live at all, and especially were they fortunate past the lot of children to be permitted to live in a flat. There were many flats in the great city, so polished and carved and burnished and be-lackeyed that children were not allowed to enter within the portals, save on visits of ceremony in charge of parents or governesses. And in one flat, where Cecil de Koven le Baron was born—just by accident and without intending any harm—he was evicted, along with his parents, by the time he reached the age where he seemed likely to be graduated from the go-cart. And yet that flat had not nearly so imposing a name as the Santa Maria.

The twenty-six children of the Santa Maria flats belonged to twenty families. All of these twenty families were peculiar, as you might learn any day by interviewing the families concerning one another. But they bore with each other's peculiarities quite cheerfully and spoke in the hall when they met. Sometimes this tolerance would even extend to conversation about the janitor, a thin creature who did the work of five men. The ladies complained that he never smiled.

"I wouldn't so much mind the hot water pipes leaking now and then," the ladies would remark in the vestibule, rustling their skirts to show that they wore silk petticoats, "if only the janitor would smile. But he looks like a cemetery."

"I know it," would be the response. "I told Mr. Wilberforce last night that if he would only get a cheerful janitor I wouldn't mind our having rubber instead of Axminster on the stairs."

"You know we were promised Axminster when we moved in," would be the plaintive response. The ladies would stand together for a moment wrapped in gloomy reflection, and then part.

The kitchen and nurse maids felt on the subject, too.

"If Carl Carlsen would only smile," they used to exclaim in sibilant whispers, as they passed on the way to the laundry. "If he'd come in an' joke while we wus washin'!"

Only Kara Johnson never said anything on the subject because she knew why Carlsen didn't smile, and was sorry for it, and would have made it all right—if it hadn't been for Lars Larsen.

Dear, dear, but this is a digression from the subject of the Lease. That terrible document was held over the heads of the children as the Herodian pronunciamento concerning small boys was over the heads of the Israelites.

It was in the Lease not to run—not to jump—not to yell. It was in the Lease not to sing in the halls, not to call from story to story, not to slide down the banisters. And there were blocks of banisters so smooth and wide and beautiful that the attraction between them and the seats of the little boy's trousers was like the attraction of a magnet for a nail. Yet not a leg, crooked or straight, fat or thin, was ever to be thrown over these polished surfaces!

It was in the Lease, too, that no peddler or agent, or suspicious stranger was to enter the Santa Maria, neither by the front door nor the back. The janitor stood in his uniform at the rear, and the lackey in his uniform at the front, to prevent any such intrusion upon the privacy of the aristocratic Santa Marias. The lackey, who politely directed people, and summoned elevators, and whistled up tubes and rang bells, thus conducting the complex social life of those favoured apartments, was not one to make a mistake, and admit any person not calculated to ornament the front parlours of the flatters.

It was this that worried the children.

For how could such a dear, disorderly, democratic rascal as the children's saint ever hope to gain a pass to that exclusive entrance and get up to the rooms of the flat children?

"You can see for yourself," said Ernest, who lived on the first floor, to Roderick who lived on the fourth, "that if Santa Claus can't get up the front stairs, and can't get up the back stairs, that all he can do is to come down the chimney. And he can't come down the chimney—at least, he can't get out of the fireplace."

"Why not?" asked Roderick, who was busy with an "all-day sucker" and not inclined to take a gloomy view of anything.

"Goosey!" cried Ernest, in great disdain. "I'll show you!" and he led Roderick, with his sucker, right into the best parlour, where the fireplace was, and showed him an awful thing.

Of course, to the ordinary observer, there was nothing awful about the fireplace. Everything in the way of bric-a-brac possessed by the Santa Maria flatters was artistic. It may have been in the Lease that only people with esthetic tastes were to be admitted to the apartments. However that may be, the fireplace, with its vases and pictures and trinkets, was something quite wonderful. Indian incense burned in a mysterious little dish, pictures of purple ladies were hung in odd corners, calendars in letters nobody could read, served to decorate, if not to educate, and glass vases of strange colours and extraordinary shapes stood about filled with roses. None of these things were awful. At least no one would have dared say they were. But what was awful was the formation of the grate. It was not a hospitable place with andirons, where noble logs of wood could be laid for the burning, nor did it have a generous iron basket where honest anthracite could glow away into the nights. Not a bit of it. It held a vertical plate of stuff that looked like dirty cotton wool, on which a tiny blue flame leaped when the gas was turned on and ignited.

"You can see for yourself!" said Ernest tragically.

Roderick could see for himself. There was an inch-wide opening down which the Friend of the Children could squeeze himself, and, as everybody knows, he needs a good deal of room now, for he has grown portly with age, and his pack every year becomes bigger, owing to the ever-increasing number of girls and boys he has to supply

"Gimini!" said Roderick, and dropped his all-day sucker on the old Bokara rug that Ernest's mamma had bought the week before at a fashionable furnishing shop, and which had given the sore throat to all the family, owing to some cunning little germs that had come over with the rug to see what American throats were like.

Oh, me, yes! but Roderick could see! Anybody could see! And a boy could see better than anybody.

"Let's go see the Telephone Boy," said Roderick. This seemed the wisest thing to do. When in doubt, all the children went to the Telephone Boy, who was the most fascinating person, with knowledge of the most wonderful kind and of a nature to throw that of Mrs. Scheherazade quite, quite in the shade—which, considering how long that loquacious lady had been a Shade, is perhaps not surprising.

The Telephone Boy knew the answers to all the conundrums in the world, and a way out of nearly all troubles such as are likely to overtake boys and girls. But now he had no suggestions to offer and could speak no comfortable words.

"He can't git inter de front, an' he can't git inter de back, an' he can't come down no chimney in dis here house, an' I tell yer dose," he said, and shut his mouth grimly, while cold apprehension crept around Ernest's heart and took the sweetness out of Roderick's sucker.

Nevertheless, hope springs eternal, and the boys each and individually asked their fathers—tremendously wise and good men—if they thought there was any hope that Santa Claus would get into the Santa Maria flats, and each of the fathers looked up from his paper and said he'd be blessed if he did!

And the words sunk deep and deep and drew the tears when the doors were closed and the soft black was all about and nobody could laugh because a boy was found crying! The girls cried too—for the awful news was whistled up tubes and whistled down tubes, till all the twenty-six flat children knew about it. The next day it was talked over in the brick court, where the children used to go to shout and race. But on this day there was neither shouting nor racing. There was, instead, a shaking of heads, a surreptitious dropping of tears, a guessing and protesting and lamenting. All the flat mothers congratulated themselves on the fact that their children were becoming so quiet and orderly, and wondered what could have come over them when they noted that they neglected to run after the patrol wagon as it whizzed round the block.

It was decided, after a solemn talk, that every child should go to its own fireplace and investigate. In the event of any fireplace being found with an opening big enough to admit Santa Claus, a note could be left directing him along the halls to the other apartments. A spirit of universal brotherhood had taken possession of the Santa Maria flatters. Misery bound them together. But the investigation proved to be disheartening. The cruel asbestos grates were everywhere. Hope lay strangled!

As time went on, melancholy settled upon the flat children. The parents noted it, and wondered if there could be sewer gas in the apartments. One over-anxious mother called in a physician, who gave the poor little child some medicine which made it quite ill. No one suspected the truth, though the children were often heard to say that it was evident that there was to be no Christmas for them! But then, what more natural for a child to say, thus hoping to win protestations—so the mothers reasoned, and let the remark pass.

The day before Christmas was gray and dismal. There was no wind—indeed, there was a sort of tightness in the air, as if the supply of freshness had given out. People had headaches—even the Telephone Boy was cross—and none of the spirit of the time appeared to enliven the flat children. There appeared to be no stir—no mystery. No whisperings went on in the corners—or at least, so it seemed to the sad babies of the Santa Maria.

"It's as plain as a monkey on a hand-organ," said the Telephone Boy to the attendants at his salon in the basement, "that there ain't to be no Christmas for we—no, not for we!"

Had not Dorothy produced, at this junction, from the folds of her fluffy silken skirts several substantial sticks of gum, there is no saying to what depths of discouragement the flat children would have fallen!

About six o'clock it seemed as if the children would smother for lack of air! It was very peculiar. Even the janitor noticed it. He spoke about it to Kara at the head of the back stairs, and she held her hand so as to let him see the new silver ring on her fourth finger, and he let go of the rope on the elevator on which he was standing and dropped to the bottom of the shaft, so that Kara sent up a wild hallo of alarm. But the janitor emerged as melancholy and unruffled as ever, only looking at his watch to see if it had been stopped by the concussion.

The Telephone Boy, who usually got a bit of something hot sent down to him from one of the tables, owing to the fact that he never ate any meal save breakfast at home, was quite forgotten on this day, and dined off two russet apples, and drew up his belt to stop the ache—for the Telephone Boy was growing very fast indeed, in spite of his poverty, and couldn't seem to stop growing somehow, although he said to himself every day that it was perfectly brutal of him to keep on that way when his mother had so many mouths to feed.

Well, well, the tightness of the air got worse. Every one was cross at dinner and complained of feeling tired afterward, and of wanting to go to bed. For all of that it was not to get to sleep, and the children tossed and tumbled for a long time before they put their little hands in the big, soft shadowy clasp of the Sandman, and trooped away after him to the happy town of sleep.

It seemed to the flat children that they had been asleep but a few moments when there came a terrible burst of wind that shook even that great house to its foundations. Actually, as they sat up in bed and called to their parents or their nurses, their voices seemed smothered with roar. Could it be that the wind was a great wild beast with a hundred tongues which licked at the roof of the building? And how many voices must it have to bellow as it did?

Sounds of falling glass, of breaking shutters, of crashing chimneys greeted their ears—not that they knew what all these sounds meant. They only knew that it seemed as if the end of the world had come. Ernest, miserable as he was, wondered if the Telephone Boy had gotten safely home, or if he were alone in the draughty room in the basement; and Roderick hugged his big brother, who slept with him and said, "Now I lay me," three times running, as fast as ever his tongue would say it.

After a terrible time the wind settled down into a steady howl like a hungry wolf, and the children went to sleep, worn out with fright and conscious that the bedclothes could not keep out the cold.

Dawn came. The children awoke, shivering. They sat up in bed and looked about them—yes, they did, the whole twenty-six of them in their different apartments and their different homes. And what do you suppose they saw—what do you suppose the twenty-six flat children saw as they looked about them?

Why, stockings, stuffed full, and trees hung full, and boxes packed full! Yes, they did! It was Christmas morning, and the bells were ringing, and all the little flat children were laughing, for Santa Claus had come! He had really come! In the wind and wild weather, while the tongues of the wind licked hungrily at the roof, while the wind howled like a hungry wolf, he had crept in somehow and laughing, no doubt, and chuckling, without question, he had filled the stockings and the trees and the boxes! Dear me, dear me, but it was a happy time! It makes me out of breath to think what a happy time it was, and how surprised the flat children were, and how they wondered how it could ever have happened.

But they found out, of course! It happened in the simplest way! Every skylight in the place was blown off and away, and that was how the wind howled so, and how the bedclothes would not keep the children warm, and how Santa Claus got in. The wind corkscrewed down into these holes, and the reckless children with their drums and dolls, their guns and toy dishes, danced around in the maelstrom and sang:

"Here's where Santa Claus came!
This is how he got in–
We should count it a sin
Yes, count it a shame,
If it hurt when he fell on the floor."

Roderick's sister, who was clever for a child of her age, and who had read Monte Cristo ten times, though she was only eleven, wrote this poem, which every one thought very fine.

And of course all the parents thought and said that Santa Claus must have jumped down the skylights. By noon there were other skylights put in, and not a sign left of the way he made his entrance—not that the way mattered a bit, no, not a bit.

Perhaps you think the Telephone Boy didn't get anything! Maybe you imagine that Santa Claus didn't get down that far. But you are mistaken. The shaft below one of the skylights went away to the bottom of the building, and it stands to reason that the old fellow must have fallen way through. At any rate there was a copy of "Tom Sawyer," and a whole plum pudding, and a number of other things, more useful but not so interesting, found down in the chilly basement room. There were, indeed.

In closing it is only proper to mention that Kara Johnson crocheted a white silk four-in-hand necktie for Carl Carlsen, the janitor—and the janitor smiled!

Little Gretchen and the Wooden Shoe

By Elizabeth Harrison

The following story is one of many which has drifted down to us from the story-loving nurseries and hearthstones of Germany. I cannot recall when I first had it told to me as a child, varied, of course, by different tellers, but always leaving that sweet, tender impression of God's loving care for the least of his children. I have since read different versions of it in at least a half-dozen story books for children.

Once upon a time, a long time ago, far away across the great ocean, in a country called Germany, there could be seen a small log hut on the edge of a great forest, whose fir-trees extended for miles and miles to the north. This little house, made of heavy hewn logs, had but one room in it. A rough pine door gave entrance to this room, and a small square window admitted the light. At the back of the house was built an old-fashioned stone chimney, out of which in winter usually curled a thin, blue smoke, showing that there was not very much fire within.

Small as the house was, it was large enough for the two people who lived in it. I want to tell you a story to-day about these two people. One was an old, gray-haired woman, so old that the little children of the village, nearly half a mile away, often wondered whether she had come into the world with the huge mountains, and the great fir-trees, which stood like giants back of her small hut. Her face was wrinkled all over with deep lines, which, if the children could only have read aright, would have told them of many years of cheerful, happy, self-sacrifice, of loving, anxious watching beside sick-beds, of quiet endurance of pain, of many a day of hunger and cold, and of a thousand deeds of unselfish love for other people; but, of course, they could not read this strange handwriting. They only knew that she was old and wrinkled, and that she stooped as she walked. None of them seemed to fear her, for her smile was always cheerful, and she had a kindly word for each of them if they chanced to meet her on her way to and from the village. With this old, old woman lived a very little girl. So bright and happy was she that the travellers who passed by the lonesome little house on the edge of the forest often thought of a sunbeam as they saw her. These two people were known in the village as Granny Goodyear and Little Gretchen.

The winter had come and the frost had snapped off many of the smaller branches from the pine-trees in the forest. Gretchen and her Granny were up by daybreak each morning. After their simple breakfast of oatmeal, Gretchen would run to the little closet and fetch Granny's old woollen shawl, which seemed almost as old as Granny herself. Gretchen always claimed the right to put the shawl over her Granny's head, even though she had to climb onto the wooden bench to do it. After carefully pinning it under Granny's chin, she gave her a good-bye kiss, and Granny started out for her morning's work in the forest. This work was nothing more nor less than the gathering up of the twigs and branches which the autumn winds and winter frosts had thrown upon the ground. These were carefully gathered into a large bundle which Granny tied together with a strong linen band. She then managed to lift the bundle to her shoulder and trudged off to the village with it. Here she sold the fagots for kindling wood to the people of the village. Sometimes she would get only a few pence each day, and sometimes a dozen or more, but on this money little Gretchen and she managed to live; they had their home, and the forest kindly furnished the wood for the fire which kept them warm in cold weather.

In the summer time Granny had a little garden at the back of the hut where she raised, with little Gretchen's help, a few potatoes and turnips and onions. These she carefully stored away for winter use. To this meagre supply, the pennies, gained by selling the twigs from the forest, added the oatmeal for Gretchen and a little black coffee for Granny. Meat was a thing they never thought of having. It cost too much money. Still, Granny and Gretchen were very happy, because they loved each other dearly. Sometimes Gretchen would be left alone all day long in the hut, because Granny would have some work to do in the village after selling her bundle of sticks and twigs. It was during these long days that little Gretchen had taught herself to sing the song which the wind sang to the pine branches. In the summer time she learned the chirp and twitter of the birds, until her voice might almost be mistaken for a bird's voice; she learned to dance as the swaying shadows did, and even to talk to the stars which shone through the little square window when Granny came home too late or too tired to talk.

Sometimes, when the weather was fine, or her Granny had an extra bundle of newly knitted stockings to take to the village, she would let little Gretchen go along with her. It chanced that one of these trips to the town came just the week before Christmas, and Gretchen's eyes were delighted by the sight of the lovely Christmas-trees which stood in the window of the village store. It seemed to her that she would never tire of looking at the knit dolls, the woolly lambs, the little wooden shops with their queer, painted men and women in them, and all the other fine things. She had never owned a plaything in her whole life; therefore, toys which you and I would not think much of, seemed to her to be very beautiful.

That night, after their supper of baked potatoes was over, and little Gretchen had cleared away the dishes and swept up the hearth, because Granny dear was so tired, she brought her own small wooden stool and placed it very near Granny's feet and sat down upon it, folding her hands on her lap. Granny knew that this meant she wanted to talk about something, so she smilingly laid away the large Bible which she had been reading, and took up her knitting, which was as much as to say: "Well, Gretchen, dear, Granny is ready to listen."

"Granny," said Gretchen slowly, "it's almost Christmas time, isn't it?"

"Yes, dearie," said Granny, "only five more days now," and then she sighed, but little Gretchen was so happy that she did not notice Granny's sigh.

"What do you think, Granny, I'll get this Christmas?" said she, looking up eagerly into Granny's face.

"Ah, child, child," said Granny, shaking her head, "you'll have no Christmas this year. We are too poor for that."

"Oh, but, Granny," interrupted little Gretchen, "think of all the beautiful toys we saw in the village to-day. Surely Santa Claus has sent enough for every little child."

"Ah, dearie," said Granny, "those toys are for people who can pay money for them, and we have no money to spend for Christmas toys."

"Well, Granny," said Gretchen, "perhaps some of the little children who live in the great house on the hill at the other end of the village will be willing to share some of their toys with me. They will be so glad to give some to a little girl who has none."

"Dear child, dear child," said Granny, leaning forward and stroking the soft, shiny hair of the little girl, "your heart is full of love. You would be glad to bring a Christmas to every child; but their heads are so full of what they are going to get that they forget all about anybody else but themselves." Then she sighed and shook her head.

"Well, Granny," said Gretchen, her bright, happy tone of voice growing a little less joyous, "perhaps the dear Santa Claus will show some of the village children how to make presents that do not cost money, and some of them may surprise me Christmas morning with a present. And, Granny, dear," added she, springing up from her low stool, "can't I gather some of the pine branches and take them to the old sick man who lives in the house by the mill, so that he can have the sweet smell of our pine forest in his room all Christmas day?"

"Yes, dearie," said Granny, "you may do what you can to make the Christmas bright and happy, but you must not expect any present yourself."

"Oh, but, Granny," said little Gretchen, her face brightening, "you forget all about the shining Christmas angels, who came down to earth and sang their wonderful song the night the beautiful Christ-Child was born! They are so loving and good that they will not forget any little child. I shall ask my dear stars to-night to tell them of us. You know," she added, with a look of relief, "the stars are so very high that they must know the angels quite well, as they come and go with their messages from the loving God."

Granny sighed, as she half whispered, "Poor child, poor child!" but Gretchen threw her arm around Granny's neck and gave her a hearty kiss, saying as she did so: "Oh, Granny, Granny, you don't talk to the stars often enough, else you wouldn't be sad at Christmas time." Then she danced all around the room, whirling her little skirts about her to show Granny how the wind had made the snow dance that day. She looked so droll and funny that Granny forgot her cares and worries and laughed with little Gretchen over her new snow-dance. The days passed on, and the morning before Christmas Eve came. Gretchen having tidied up the little room—for Granny had taught her to be a careful little housewife—was off to the forest, singing a birdlike song, almost as happy and free as the birds themselves. She was very busy that day, preparing a surprise for Granny. First, however, she gathered the most beautiful of the fir branches within her reach to take the next morning to the old sick man who lived by the mill. The day was all too short for the happy little girl. When Granny came trudging wearily home that night, she found the frame of the doorway covered with green pine branches.

"It's to welcome you, Granny! It's to welcome you!" cried Gretchen;"our old dear home wanted to give you a Christmas welcome. Don't you see, the branches of evergreen make it look as if it were smiling all over, and it is trying to say, 'A happy Christmas' to you, Granny!"

Granny laughed and kissed the little girl, as they opened the door and went in together. Here was a new surprise for Granny. The four posts of the wooden bed, which stood in one corner of the room, had been trimmed by the busy little fingers, with smaller and more flexible branches of the pine-trees. A small bouquet of red mountain-ash berries stood at each side of the fireplace, and these, together with the trimmed posts of the bed, gave the plain old room quite a festival look. Gretchen laughed and clapped her hands and danced about until the house seemed full of music to poor, tired Granny, whose heart had been sad as she turned toward their home that night, thinking of the disappointment which must come to loving little Gretchen the next morning.

After supper was over little Gretchen drew her stool up to Granny's side, and laying her soft, little hands on Granny's knee, asked to be told once again the story of the coming of the Christ-Child; how the night that he was born the beautiful angels had sung their wonderful song, and how the whole sky had become bright with a strange and glorious light, never seen by the people of earth before. Gretchen had heard the story many, many times before, but she never grew tired of it, and now that Christmas Eve had come again, the happy little child wanted to hear it once more.

When Granny had finished telling it the two sat quiet and silent for a little while thinking it over; then Granny rose and said that it was time for them to go to bed. She slowly took off her heavy wooden shoes, such as are worn in that country, and placed them beside the hearth. Gretchen looked thoughtfully at them for a minute or two, and then she said, "Granny, don't you think that somebody in all this wide world will think of us to-night?"

"Nay, Gretchen," said Granny, "I don't think any one will."

"Well, then, Granny," said Gretchen, "the Christmas angels will, I know; so I am going to take one of your wooden shoes, and put it on the windowsill outside, so that they may see it as they pass by. I am sure the stars will tell the Christmas angels where the shoe is."

"Ah, you foolish, foolish child," said Granny, "you are only getting ready for a disappointment To-morrow morning there will be nothing whatever in the shoe. I can tell you that now."

But little Gretchen would not listen. She only shook her head and cried out: "Ah, Granny, you don't talk enough to the stars." With this she seized the shoe, and, opening the door, hurried out to place it on the windowsill. It was very dark without, and something soft and cold seemed to gently kiss her hair and face. Gretchen knew by this that it was snowing, and she looked up to the sky, anxious to see if the stars were in sight, but a strong wind was tumbling the dark, heavy snow-clouds about and had shut away all else.

"Never mind," said Gretchen softly to herself, "the stars are up there, even if I can't see them, and the Christmas angels do not mind snowstorms."

Just then a rough wind went sweeping by the little girl, whispering something to her which she could not understand, and then it made a sudden rush up to the snow-clouds and parted them, so that the deep, mysterious sky appeared beyond, and shining down out of the midst of it was Gretchen's favourite star.

"Ah, little star, little star!" said the child, laughing aloud, "I knew you were there, though I couldn't see you. Will you whisper to the Christmas angels as they come by that little Gretchen wants so very much to have a Christmas gift to-morrow morning, if they have one to spare, and that she has put one of Granny's shoes upon the windowsill ready for it?"

A moment more and the little girl, standing on tiptoe, had reached the windowsill and placed the shoe upon it, and was back again in the house beside Granny and the warm fire.

The two went quietly to bed, and that night as little Gretchen knelt to pray to the Heavenly Father, she thanked him for having sent the Christ-Child into the world to teach all mankind how to be loving and unselfish, and in a few moments she was quietly sleeping, dreaming of the Christmas angels.

The next morning, very early, even before the sun was up, little Gretchen was awakened by the sound of sweet music coming from the village. She listened for a moment and then she knew that the choir-boys were singing the Christmas carols in the open air of the village street. She sprang up out of bed and began to dress herself as quickly as possible, singing as she dressed. While Granny was slowly putting on her clothes, little Gretchen, having finished dressing herself, unfastened the door and hurried out to see what the Christmas angels had left in the old wooden shoe.

The white snow covered everything—trees, stumps, roads, and pastures—until the whole world looked like fairyland. Gretchen climbed up on a large stone which was beneath the window and carefully lifted down the wooden shoe. The snow tumbled off of it in a shower over the little girl's hands, but she did not heed that; she ran hurriedly back into the house, putting her hand into the toe of the shoe as she ran.

"Oh, Granny! Oh, Granny!" she exclaimed, "you didn't believe the Christmas angels would think about us, but see, they have, they have! Here is a dear little bird nestled down in the toe of your shoe! Oh, isn't he beautiful?"

Granny came forward and looked at what the child was holding lovingly in her hand. There she saw a tiny chick-a-dee, whose wing was evidently broken by the rough and boisterous winds of the night before, and who had taken shelter in the safe, dry toe of the old wooden shoe. She gently took the little bird out of Gretchen's hands, and skilfully bound his broken wing to his side, so that he need not hurt himself by trying to fly with it. Then she showed Gretchen how to make a nice warm nest for the little stranger, close beside the fire, and when their breakfast was ready she let Gretchen feed the little bird with a few moist crumbs.

Later in the day Gretchen carried the fresh, green boughs to the old sick man by the mill, and on her way home stopped to see and enjoy the Christmas toys of some other children whom she knew, never once wishing that they were hers. When she reached home she found that the little bird had gone to sleep. Soon, however, he opened his eyes and stretched his head up, saying just as plain as a bird could say, "Now, my new friends, I want you to give me something more to eat." Gretchen gladly fed him again, and then, holding him in her lap, she softly and gently stroked his gray feathers until the little creature seemed to lose all fear of her. That evening Granny taught her a Christmas hymn and told her another beautiful Christmas story. Then Gretchen made up a funny little story to tell to the birdie. He winked his eyes and turned his head from side to side in such a droll fashion that Gretchen laughed until the tears came.

As Granny and she got ready for bed that night, Gretchen put her arms softly around Granny's neck, and whispered: "What a beautiful Christmas we have had to-day, Granny! Is there anything in the world more lovely than Christmas?"

"Nay, child, nay," said Granny, "not to such loving hearts as yours."

The Pine Tree

By Hans Christian Andersen

I. WHEN IT WAS LITTLE

Out in the woods stood such a nice little Pine Tree: he had a good place; the sun could get at him; there was fresh air enough; and round him grew many big comrades, both pines and firs. But the little Pine wanted so very much to be a grown-up tree.

He did not think of the warm sun and of the fresh air, he did not care for the little cottage-children who ran about and prattled when they were looking for wild strawberries and raspberries. Often they came with a whole jug full, or had their strawberries strung on a straw, and sat down near the little Tree and said, "Oh, what a nice little fellow!" This was what the Tree could not bear to hear.

The year after he had shot up a good deal, and the next year after he was still bigger; for with pine trees one can always tell by the shoots how many years old they are.

"Oh, were I but such a big tree as the others are," sighed the little Tree. "Then I could spread my branches so far, and with the tops look out into the wide world! Birds would build nests among my branches; and when there was a breeze, I could nod as grandly as the others there."

He had no delight at all in the sunshine, or in the birds, or the red clouds which morning and evening sailed above him.

When now it was winter and the snow all around lay glittering white, a hare would often come leaping along, and jump right over the little Tree. Oh, that made him so angry! But two winters went by, and with the third the Tree was so big that the hare had to go round it. "Oh, to grow, to grow, to become big and old, and be tall," thought the Tree: "that, after all, is the most delightful thing in the world!"

In autumn the wood-cutters always came and felled some of the largest trees. This happened every year, and the young Pine Tree, that was now quite well grown, trembled at the sight; for the great stately trees fell to the earth with noise and cracking, the branches were lopped off, and the trees looked quite bare, they were so long and thin; you would hardly know them for trees, and then they were laid on carts, and horses dragged them out of the wood.

Where did they go to? What became of them?

In spring, when the Swallow and the Stork came, the Tree asked them, "Don't you know where they have been taken? Have you not met them anywhere?"

The Swallow did not know anything about it; but the Stork looked doubtful, nodded his head, and said, "Yes; I have it; I met many new ships as I was flying from Egypt; on the ships were splendid masts, and I dare say it was they that smelt so of pine. I wish you joy, for they lifted themselves on high in fine style!"

"Oh, were I but old enough to fly across the sea! How does the sea really look? and what is it like?"

"Aye, that takes a long time to tell," said the Stork, and away he went.

"Rejoice in thy youth!" said the Sunbeams, "rejoice in thy hearty growth, and in the young life that is in thee!"

And the Wind kissed the Tree, and the Dew wept tears over him, but the Pine Tree understood it not.

II. CHRISTMAS IN THE WOODS

When Christmas came, quite young trees were cut down; trees which were not even so large or of the same age as this Pine Tree, who had no rest or peace, but always wanted to be off. These young trees, and they were always the finest looking, always kept their branches; they were laid on carts, and the horses drew them out of the wood.

"Where are they going to?" asked the Pine Tree. "They are not taller than I; there was one, indeed, that was much shorter;—and why do they keep all their branches? Where are they carrying them to?"

"We know! we know!" chirped the Sparrows. "We have peeped in at the windows down there in the town. We know where they are carrying them to. Oh, they are going to where it is as bright and splendid as you can think! We peeped through the windows, and saw them planted in the middle of the warm room, and dressed with the most splendid things,—with gilded apples, with gingerbread, with toys and many hundred lights!"

"And then?" asked the Pine Tree, and he trembled in every bough. "And then? What happens then?"

"We did not see anything more: it beat everything!"

"I wonder if I am to sparkle like that!" cried the Tree, rejoicing. "That is still better than to go over the sea! How I do suffer for very longing! Were Christmas but come! I am now tall, and stretch out like the others that were carried off last year! Oh, if I were already on the cart! I wish I were in the warm room with all the splendor and brightness. And then? Yes; then will come something better, something still grander, or why should they dress me out so? There must come something better, something still grander,—but what? Oh, how I long, how I suffer! I do not know myself what is the matter with me!"

"Rejoice in us!" said the Air and the Sunlight; "rejoice in thy fresh youth out here in the open air!"

But the Tree did not rejoice at all; he grew and grew; and he stood there in all his greenery; rich green was he winter and summer. People that saw him said, "That's a fine tree!" and toward Christmas he was the first that was cut down. The axe struck deep into the very pith; the Tree fell to the earth with a sigh: he felt a pang—it was like a swoon; he could not think of happiness, for he was sad at being parted from his home, from the place where he had sprung up. He well knew that he should never see his dear old comrades, the little bushes and flowers around him, any more; perhaps not even the birds! The setting off was not at all pleasant.

The Tree only came to himself when he was unloaded in a courtyard with other trees, and heard a man say, "That one is splendid! we don't want the others." Then two servants came in rich livery and carried the Pine Tree into a large and splendid room. Portraits were hanging on the walls, and near the white porcelain stove stood two large Chinese vases with lions on the covers. There, too, were large easy-chairs, silken sofas, large tables full of picture-books, and full of toys worth a hundred times a hundred dollars—at least so the children said. And the Pine Tree was stuck upright in a cask filled with sand: but no one could see that it was a cask, for green cloth was hung all around it, and it stood on a gayly colored carpet. Oh, how the Tree quivered! What was to happen? The servants, as well as the young ladies, dressed it. On one branch there hung little nets cut out of colored paper; each net was filled with sugar-plums; gilded apples and walnuts hung as though they grew tightly there, and more than a hundred little red, blue, and white tapers were stuck fast into the branches. Dolls that looked for all the world like men—the Tree had never seen such things before—fluttered among the leaves, and at the very top a large star of gold tinsel was fixed. It was really splendid—splendid beyond telling.

"This evening!" said they all; "how it will shine this evening!"

"Oh," thought the Tree, "if it were only evening! If the tapers were but lighted! And then I wonder what will happen! I wonder if the other trees from the forest will come to look at me! I wonder if the sparrows will beat against the window-panes! I wonder if I shall take root here, and stand dressed so winter and summer!"

Aye, aye, much he knew about the matter! but he had a real back-ache for sheer longing, and a back-ache with trees is the same thing as a head-ache with us.

III. CHRISTMAS IN THE HOUSE

The candles were now lighted. What brightness! What splendor! The Tree trembled so in every bough that one of the tapers set fire to a green branch. It blazed up splendidly.

Now the Tree did not even dare to tremble. That was a fright! He was so afraid of losing something of all his finery, that he was quite confused amidst the glare and brightness; and now both folding-doors opened, and a troop of children rushed in as if they would tip the whole Tree over. The older folks came quietly behind; the little ones stood quite still, but only for a moment, then they shouted so that the whole place echoed their shouts, they danced round the Tree, and one present after another was pulled off.

"What are they about?" thought the Tree. "What is to happen now?" And the lights burned down to the very branches, and as they burned down they were put out one after the other, and then the children had leave to plunder the Tree. Oh, they rushed upon it so that it cracked in all its limbs; if its tip-top with the gold star on it had not been fastened to the ceiling, it would have tumbled over.

The children danced about with their pretty toys; no one looked at the Tree except the old nurse, who peeped in among the branches; but it was only to see if there was a fig or an apple that had been forgotten.

"A story! a story!" cried the children, and they dragged a little fat man toward the Tree. He sat down under it, and said, "Now we are in the shade, and the Tree can hear very well too. But I shall tell only one story. Now which will you have: that about Ivedy-Avedy, or about Klumpy-Dumpy who tumbled downstairs, and came to the throne after all, and married the princess?"

"Ivedy-Avedy," cried some; "Klumpy-Dumpy," cried the others. There was such a bawling and screaming!—the Pine Tree alone was silent, and he thought to himself, "Am I not to bawl with the rest?—am I to do nothing whatever?"—for he was one of them, and he had done what he had to do.

And the man told about Klumpy-Dumpy who tumbled downstairs, and came to the throne after all, and married the princess. And the children clapped their hands, and cried out, "Go on, go on!" They wanted to hear about Ivedy-Avedy too, but the little man only told them about Klumpy-Dumpy. The Pine Tree stood quite still and thoughtful: the birds in the wood had never told anything like this. "Klumpy-Dumpy fell downstairs, and yet he married the princess! Yes, yes, that's the way of the world!" thought the Pine Tree, and he believed it all, because it was such a nice man who told the story.

"Well, well! who knows, perhaps I may fall downstairs, too, and so get a princess!" And he looked forward with joy to the next day when he should be decked out with lights and toys, fruits and tinsel.

"To-morrow I won't tremble!" thought the Pine Tree. "I will enjoy to the full all my splendor! To-morrow I shall hear again the story of Klumpy-Dumpy, and perhaps that of Ivedy-Avedy too." And the whole night the Tree stood still in deep thought.

In the morning the servant and the maid came in.

IV. IN THE ATTIC

"Now all the finery will begin again," thought the Pine. But they dragged him out of the room, and up the stairs into the attic; and here in a dark corner, where no daylight could enter, they left him. "What's the meaning of this?" thought the Tree. "What am I to do here? What shall I see and hear now, I wonder?" And he leaned against the wall and stood and thought and thought. And plenty of time he had, for days and nights passed, and nobody came up; and when at last somebody did come, it was only to put some great trunks in the corner. There stood the Tree quite hidden; it seemed as if he had been entirely forgotten.

"'T is now winter out-of-doors!" thought the Tree. "The earth is hard and covered with snow; men cannot plant me now; therefore I have been put up here under cover till spring! How thoughtful that is! How good men are, after all! If it were not so dark here, and so terribly lonely! Not even a hare. Out there it was so pleasant in the woods, when the snow was on the ground, and the hare leaped by; yes—even when he jumped over me; but I did not like it then. It is terribly lonely here!"

"Squeak! squeak!" said a little Mouse at the same moment, peeping out of his hole. And then another little one came. They snuffed about the Pine Tree, and rustled among the branches.

"It is dreadfully cold," said the little Mouse. "But for that, it would be delightful here, old Pine, wouldn't it!"

"I am by no means old," said the Pine Tree. "There are many a good deal older than I am."

"Where do you come from?" asked the Mice; "and what can you do?" They were so very curious. "Tell us about the most beautiful spot on earth. Have you been there? Were you ever in the larder, where cheeses lie on the shelves, and hams hang from above; where one dances about on tallow candles; where one goes in lean and comes out fat?"

"I don't know that place," said the Tree. "But I know the wood where the sun shines, and where the little birds sing."

And then he told his story from his youth up; and the little Mice had never heard the like before; and they listened and said, "Well, to be sure! How much you have seen! How happy you must have been!"

"I!" said the Pine Tree, and he thought over what he had himself told. "Yes, really those were happy times." And then he told about Christmas Eve, when he was decked out with cakes and candles.

"Oh," said the little Mice, "how lucky you have been, old Pine Tree!"

"I am not at all old," said he. "I came from the wood this winter; I am in my prime, and am only rather short of my age."

"What delightful stories you know!" said the Mice: and the next night they came with four other little Mice, who were to hear what the Tree had to tell; and the more he told, the more plainly he remembered all himself; and he thought: "That was a merry time! But it can come! it can come! Klumpy-Dumpy fell down stairs, and yet he got a princess! Maybe I can get a princess too!" And all of a sudden he thought of a nice little Birch Tree growing out in the woods: to the Pine, that would be a really charming princess.

"Who is Klumpy-Dumpy?" asked the little Mice.

So then the Pine Tree told the whole fairy tale, for he could remember every single word of it; and the little Mice jumped for joy up to the very top of the Tree. Next night two more Mice came, and on Sunday two Rats, even; but they said the stories were not amusing, which vexed the little Mice, because they, too, now began to think them not so very amusing either.

"Do you know only that one story?" asked the Rats.

"Only that one!" answered the Tree. "I heard it on my happiest evening; but I did not then know how happy I was."

"It is a very stupid story! Don't you know one about bacon and tallow candles? Can't you tell any larder-stories?"

"No," said the Tree.

"Thank you, then," said the Rats; and they went home.

At last the little Mice stayed away also; and the Tree sighed: "After all, it was very pleasant when the sleek little Mice sat round me and heard what I told them. Now that too is over. But I will take good care to enjoy myself when I am brought out again."

But when was that to be? Why, it was one morning when there came a number of people and set to work in the loft. The trunks were moved, the tree was pulled out and thrown down; they knocked him upon the floor, but a man drew him at once toward the stairs, where the daylight shone.

V. OUT OF DOORS AGAIN

"Now life begins again," thought the Tree. He felt the fresh air, the first sunbeam,—and now he was out in the courtyard. All passed so quickly that the Tree quite forgot to look to himself, there was so much going on around him. The court adjoined a garden, and all was in flower; the roses hung over the fence, so fresh and smelling so sweetly; the lindens were in blossom, the Swallows flew by, and said, "Quirre-virre-vit! my husband is come!" But it was not the Pine Tree that they meant.

"Now, I shall really live," said he with joy, and spread out his branches; dear! dear! they were all dry and yellow. It was in a corner among weeds and nettles that he lay. The golden star of tinsel was still on top of the Tree, and shone in the bright sunshine.

In the courtyard a few of the merry children were playing who had danced at Christmas round the Tree, and were so glad at the sight of him. One of the littlest ran and tore off the golden star.

"See what is still on the ugly old Christmas Tree!" said he, and he trampled on the branches, so that they cracked under his feet.

And the Tree saw all the beauty of the flowers, and the freshness in the garden; he saw himself, and he wished he had stayed in his dark corner in the attic: he thought of his fresh youth in the wood, of the merry Christmas Eve, and of the little Mice who had heard so gladly the story of Klumpy-Dumpy.

"Gone! gone!" said the poor Tree. "Had I but been happy when I could be. Gone! gone!"

And the gardener's boy came and chopped the Tree into small pieces; there was a whole heap lying there. The wood flamed up finely under the large brewing kettle, and it sighed so deeply! Each sigh was like a little shot. So the children ran to where it lay and sat down before the fire, and peeped in at the blaze, and shouted "Piff! paff!" But at every snap there was a deep sigh. The Tree was thinking of summer days in the wood, and of winter nights when the stars shone; it was thinking of Christmas Eve and Klumpy-Dumpy, the only fairy tale it had heard and knew how to tell,—and so the Tree burned out.

The boys played about in the court, and the youngest wore the gold star on his breast which the Tree had worn on the happiest evening of his life. Now, that was gone, the Tree was gone, and gone too was the story. All, all was gone, and that's the way with all stories.

The Thunder Oak

By William Walsh

A Scandinavian Legend

When the heathen raged through the forests of the ancient Northland there grew a giant tree branching with huge limbs toward the clouds. It was the Thunder Oak of the war-god Thor.

Thither, under cover of night, heathen priests were wont to bring their victims—both men and beasts—and slay them upon the altar of the thunder-god. There in the darkness was wrought many an evil deed, while human blood was poured forth and watered the roots of that gloomy tree, from whose branches depended the mistletoe, the fateful plant that sprang from the blood-fed veins of the oak. So gloomy and terror-ridden was the spot on which grew the tree that no beasts of field or forest would lodge beneath its dark branches, nor would birds nest or perch among its gnarled limbs.

Long, long ago, on a white Christmas Eve, Thor's priests held their winter rites beneath the Thunder Oak. Through the deep snow of the dense forest hastened throngs of heathen folk, all intent on keeping the mystic feast of the mighty Thor. In the hush of the night the folk gathered in the glade where stood the tree. Closely they pressed around the great altar-stone under the overhanging boughs where stood the white-robed priests. Clearly shone the moonlight on all.

Then from the altar flashed upward the sacrificial flames, casting their lurid glow on the straining faces of the human victims awaiting the blow of the priest's knife.

But the knife never fell, for from the silent avenues of the dark forest came the good Saint Winfred and his people. Swiftly the saint drew from his girdle a shining axe. Fiercely he smote the Thunder Oak, hewing a deep gash in its trunk. And while the heathen folk gazed in horror and wonder, the bright blade of the axe circled faster and faster around Saint Winfred's head, and the flakes of wood flew far and wide from the deepening cut in the body of the tree.

Suddenly there was heard overhead the sound of a mighty, rushing wind. A whirling blast struck the tree. It gripped the oak from its foundations. Backward it fell like a tower, groaning as it split into four pieces.

But just behind it, unharmed by the ruin, stood a young fir tree, pointing its green spire to heaven.

Saint Winfred dropped his axe, and turned to speak to the people. Joyously his voice rang out through the crisp, winter air:—

"This little tree, a young child of the forest, shall be your holy tree to-night. It is the tree of peace, for your houses are built of fir. It is the sign of endless life, for its leaves are forever green. See how it points upward to heaven! Let this be called the tree of the Christ Child. Gather about it, not in the wildwood, but in your own homes. There it will shelter no deeds of blood, but loving gifts and rites of kindness. So shall the peace of the White Christ reign in your hearts!"

And with songs of joy the multitude of heathen folk took up the little fir tree and bore it to the house of their chief, and there with good will and peace they kept the holy Christmastide.

THE CHRISTMAS THORN OF GLASTONBURY

Adapted from William of Malmesbury

A Legend of Ancient Britain

There is a golden Christmas legend and it relates how Joseph of Arimathea—that good man and just, who laid our Lord in his own sepulcher, was persecuted by Pontius Pilate, and how he fled from Jerusalem carrying with him the Holy Grail hidden beneath a cloth of samite, mystical and white.

For many moons he wandered, leaning on his staff cut from a white-thorn bush. He passed over raging seas and dreary wastes, he wandered through trackless forests, climbed rugged mountains, and forded many floods. At last he came to Gaul where the Apostle Philip was preaching the glad tidings to the heathen. And there Joseph abode for a little space.

Now, upon a night while Joseph lay asleep in his hut, he was wakened by a radiant light. And as he gazed with wondering eyes he saw an angel standing by his couch, wrapped in a cloud of incense.

"Joseph of Arimathea," said the angel, "cross thou over into Britain and preach the glad tidings to King Arvigarus. And there, where a Christmas miracle shall come to pass, do thou build the first Christian church in that land."

And while Joseph lay perplexed and wondering in his heart what answer he should make, the angel vanished from his sight.

Then Joseph left his hut and calling the Apostle Philip, gave him the angel's message. And, when morning dawned, Philip sent him on his way, accompanied by eleven chosen followers. To the water's side they went, and embarking in a little ship, they came unto the coasts of Britain.

And they were met there by the heathen who carried them before Arvigarus their king. To him and to his people did Joseph of Arimathea preach the glad tidings; but the king's heart, though moved, was not convinced. Nevertheless he gave to Joseph and his followers Avalon, the happy isle, the isle of the blessed, and he bade them depart straightway and build there an altar to their God.

And a wonderful gift was this same Avalon, sometimes called the Island of Apples, and also known to the people of the land as Ynis-witren, the Isle of Glassy Waters. Beautiful and peaceful was it. Deep it lay in the midst of a green valley, and the balmy breezes fanned its apple orchards, and scattered afar the sweet fragrance of rosy blossoms or ripened fruit. Soft grew the green grass beneath the feet. The smooth waves gently lapped the shore, and water-lilies floated on the surface of the tide; while in the blue sky above sailed the fleecy clouds.

And it was on the holy Christmas Eve that Joseph and his companions reached the Isle of Avalon. With them they carried the Holy Grail hidden beneath its cloth of snow-white samite. Heavily they toiled up the steep ascent of the hill called Weary-All. And when they reached the top Joseph thrust his thorn-staff into the ground.

And, lo! a miracle! the thorn-staff put forth roots, sprouted and budded, and burst into a mass of white and fragrant flowers! And on the spot where the thorn had bloomed, there Joseph built the first Christian church in Britain. And he made it "wattled all round" of osiers gathered from the water's edge. And in the chapel they placed the Holy Grail.

And so, it is said, ever since at Glastonbury Abbey—the name by which that Avalon is known to-day—on Christmas Eve the white thorn buds and blooms.

Widow Townsend's Visitor

By Anonymous

The fire crackled cheerfully on the broad hearth of an old-fashioned fireplace in an old-fashioned public house in an old fashioned village, down in that part of the Old Dominion called the "Eastern Shore." A cat and three kittens basked in the warmth, and a decrepit yellow dog, lying full in the reflection of the blaze, wrinkled his black nose approvingly, as he turned his hind feet where his fore feet had been. Over the chimney hung several fine hams and pieces of dried beef. Apples were festooned along the ceiling, and other signs of plenty and good cheer were scattered profusely about. There were plants, too, on the window ledges, horse-shoe geraniums, and dew-plants, and a monthly rose, just budding, to say nothing of pots of violets that perfumed the whole place whenever they took it into their purple heads to bloom. The floor was carefully swept, the chairs had not a speck of dust upon leg or round, the long settle near the fireplace shone as if it had been just varnished, and the eight-day clock in the corner had had its white face newly washed, and seemed determined to tick the louder for it.

Two arm-chairs were drawn up at cozy distance from the hearth and each other; a candle, a newspaper, a pair of spectacles, a dish of red cheeked apples, and a pitcher of cider, filled a little table between them. In one of these chairs sat a comfortable-looking woman about forty-five, with cheeks as red as the apples, and eyes as dark and bright as they had ever been, resting her elbow on the table and her head upon her hand, and looking thoughtfully into the fire.

This was Widow Townsend, "relict" of Mr. Levi Townsend, who had been mouldering into dust in the neighboring churchyard for seven years and more. She was thinking of her dead husband, possibly because all her work being done, and the servant gone to bed, the sight of his empty chair at the other side of the table, and the silence of the room, made her a little lonely.

"Seven years," so the widow's reverie ran;"it seems as if it were more than fifty, and Christmas nigh here again, and yet I don't look so very old neither. Perhaps it's not having any children to bother my life out, as other people have. They may say what they like—children are more plague than profit, that's my opinion. Look at my sister Jerusha, with her six boys. She's worn to a shadow, and I am sure they have done it, though she never will own it."

The widow took an apple from the dish and began to peel it.

"How fond Mr. Townsend used to be of these apples! He'll never eat any more of them, poor fellow, for I don't suppose they have apples where he has gone to. Heigho! I remember very well how I used to throw apple-peel over my head when I was a girl to see who I was going to marry."

Mrs. Townsend stopped short and blushed, for in those days she did not know Mr. T., and was always looking eagerly to see if the peel had formed a capital S. Her meditations took a new turn.

"How handsome Sam Payson was, and how much I use to care about him! I wonder what has become of him! Jerusha says he went away from our village just after I did, and no one has ever heard of him since. What a silly thing that quarrel was! If it had not been for that—"

Here came a long pause, during which the widow looked very steadfastly at the empty [Pg 212]arm-chair of Levi Townsend, deceased. Her fingers played carelessly with the apple-peel: she drew it safely towards her, and looked around the room.

"Upon my word, it is very ridiculous, and I don't know what the neighbors would say if they saw me."

Still the plump fingers drew the red peel nearer.

"But then they can't see me, that's a comfort; and the cat and old Bose never will know what it means. Of course I don't *believe* anything about it."

The peel hung gracefully from her hand.

"But still, I should like to try; it would seem like old times, and—"

Over her head it went, and curled up quietly on the floor at a little distance. Old Bose, who always slept with one eye open, saw it fall, and marched deliberately up to smell it.

"Bose—Bose—don't touch!" cried his mistress, and bending over it with beating heart, she turned as red as fire. There was as handsome a capital S as any one could wish to see.

A great knock came suddenly at the door. Bose growled, and the widow screamed and snatched up the apple-peel.

"It's Mr. T.—it's his spirit come back again, because I tried that silly trick," she thought fearfully to herself.

Another knock—louder than the first, and a man's voice exclaimed:

"Hello—the house!"

"Who is it?" asked the widow, somewhat relieved to find that the departed Levi was still safe in his grave on the hillside.

"A stranger," said the voice.

"What do you want?"

"To get a lodging here for the night."

The widow deliberated.

"Can't you go on? There's a house half a mile farther, if you keep to the right-hand side of the road, and turn to the left after you get by—"

"It's raining cats and dogs, and I'm very delicate," said the stranger, coughing. "I'm wet to the skin: don't you think you can accommodate me?—I don't mind sleeping on the floor."

"Raining, is it? I didn't know that," and the kind-hearted little woman unbarred the door very quickly. "Come in, whoever you may be; I only asked you to go on because I am a lone woman, with only one servant in the house."

The stranger entered, shaking himself like a Newfoundland dog upon the step, and scattering a little shower of drops over his hostess and her nicely swept floor.

"Ah, that looks comfortable after a man has been out for hours in a storm," he said, as he caught sight of the fire; and striding along toward the hearth, followed by Bose, who sniffed suspiciously at his heels, he stationed himself in the arm-chair—*Mr. Townsend's arm-chair*! which had been kept "sacred to his memory" for seven years. The widow was horrified, but her guest looked so weary and worn-out that she could not ask him to move, but busied herself in stirring up the blaze that he might the sooner dry his dripping clothes.

A new thought struck her: Mr. T. had worn a comfortable dressing-gown during his illness, which still hung in the closet at her right. She could not let this poor man catch his death, by sitting in that wet coat. If he was in Mr. Townsend's chair, why should he not be in Mr. Townsend's wrapper? She went nimbly to the closet, took it down, fished out a pair of slippers from a boot-rack below, and brought them to him.

"I think you had better take off your coat and boots—you will have the rheumatic fever, or[Pg 214] something like it, if you don't. Here are some things for you to wear while they are drying. And you must be hungry, too; I will go into the pantry and get you something to eat."

She bustled away, "on hospitable thoughts intent," and the stranger made the exchange with a quizzical smile playing around his lips. He was a tall, well-formed man, with a bold but handsome face, sun-burned and heavily bearded, and looking anything but "delicate," though his blue eyes glanced out from under a forehead as white as snow. He looked around the kitchen with a mischievous air, and stretched out his feet decorated with the defunct Boniface's slippers.

"Upon my word, this is stepping into the old man's shoes with a vengeance! And what a hearty, good-humored looking woman she is! Kind as a kitten," and he leaned forward and stroked the cat and her brood, and then patted old Bose upon the head. The widow, bringing in sundry good things, looked pleased at his attention to her dumb friends.

"It's a wonder Bose does not growl; he generally does if strangers touch him. Dear me, how stupid!"

The last remark was neither addressed to the stranger nor to the dog but to herself She had forgotten that the little stand was not empty, and there was no room on it for the things she held.

"Oh, I'll manage it," said her guest, gathering up paper, candle, apples, and spectacles (it was not without a little pang that she saw them in his hand, for they had been her husband's, and were placed each night, like the arm-chair, beside her) and depositing them on the settle.

"Give me the table-cloth, ma'am, I can spread it as well as any woman; I've learned that along with scores of other things, in my wanderings. Now let me relieve you of those dishes; they are[Pg 215] far too heavy for those hands"—the widow blushed;"and now please, sit down with me, or I cannot eat a morsel."

"I had supper long ago, but really I think I can take something more," said Mrs. Townsend, drawing her chair nearer to the table.

"Of course you can, my dear lady; in this cold fall weather people ought to eat twice as much as they do in warm. Let me give you a piece of this ham, your own curing, I dare say."

"Yes: my poor husband was very fond of it. He used to say that no one understood curing ham and drying beef better than I."

"He was a most sensible man, I am sure. I drink your health, ma'am, in this cider."

He took a long draught, and set down his glass.

"It is like nectar."

The widow was feeding Bose and the cat (who thought they were entitled to a share of every meal eaten in the house), and did not quite hear what he said.

"Fine dog, ma'am, and a very pretty cat."

"They were my husband's favorites," and a sigh followed the answer.

"Ah, your husband must have been a very happy man."

The blue eyes looked at her so long, that she grew flurried.

"Is there anything more I can get for you, sir?" she asked, at last.

"Nothing, thank you; I have finished."

She rose to clear the things away. He assisted her, and somehow their hands had a queer knack of touching as they carried the dishes to the pantry shelves. Coming back to the kitchen, she put the apples and cider in their old places, and brought out a clean pipe and a box of tobacco from an arched recess near the chimney.

"My husband always said he could not sleep[Pg 216] after eating supper late unless he smoked," she said. "Perhaps you would like to try it."

"Not if it is to drive you away," he answered, for she had her candle in her hand.

"Oh, no; I do not object to smoke at all." She put the candle down; some faint suggestion about "propriety" troubled her, but she glanced at the old clock, and felt reassured. It was only half-past nine.

The stranger pushed the stand back after the pipe was lit, and drew her easy-chair a little nearer the fire, and his own.

"Come, sit down," he said, pleadingly;"it's not late, and when a man has been knocking about in California and all sorts of places, for a score of years, he is glad enough to get into a berth like this, and to have a pretty woman to speak to once again."

"California! Have you been in California?" she exclaimed, dropping into the chair at once. Unconsciously, she had long cherished the idea that Sam Payson, the lover of her youth, with whom she had so foolishly quarreled, had pitched his tent, after many wanderings, in that far-off land. Her heart warmed to one who, with something of Sam's looks and ways about him, had also been sojourning in that country, and who very possibly had met him—perhaps had known him intimately! At that thought her heart beat quick, and she looked very graciously at the bearded stranger, who, wrapped in Mr. Townsend's dressing-gown, wearing Mr. Townsend's slippers, and sitting in Mr. Townsend's chair, beside Mr. Townsend's wife, smoked Mr. Townsend's pipe with such an air of feeling most thoroughly and comfortably at home!

"Yes, ma'am. I've been in California for the last six years. And before that I went quite round the world in a whaling ship!"

"Good gracious!"

The stranger sent a puff of smoke curling gracefully over his head.

"It's very strange, my dear lady, how often you see one thing as you go wandering about the world after that fashion."

"And what is that?"

"Men, without house or home above their heads, roving here and there, and turning up in all sorts of odd places; caring very little for life as a general thing, and making fortunes just to fling them away again, and all for one reason. You don't ask me what *that* is? No doubt you know already very well."

"I think not, sir."

"Because a woman has jilted them!"

Here was a long pause, and Mr. Townsend's pipe emitted short puffs with surprising rapidity. A guilty conscience needs no accuser, and the widow's cheek was dyed with blushes as she thought of the absent Sam.

"I wonder how women manage when *they* get served in the same way," said the stranger musingly;"you never meet *them* roaming up and down in that style."

"No," said Mrs. Townsend, with some spirit, "if a woman is in trouble she must stay at home and bear it, the best way she can. And there's more women bearing such things than we know of, I dare say."

"Like enough. We never know whose hand gets pinched in a trap unless they scream. And women are too shy or too sensible—which you choose—for that."

"Did you ever, in all your wanderings, meet any one by the name of Samuel Payson?" asked the widow, unconcernedly.

The stranger looked toward her; she was rummaging the table-drawer for her knitting work,[Pg 218] and did not notice him. When it was found, and the needles in motion, he answered her.

"Payson—Sam Payson? Why, he was my most intimate friend! Do you know him?"

"A little—that is, I used to, when I was a girl. Where did you meet him?"

"He went with me on the whaling voyage I told you of, and afterward to California. We had a tent together, and some other fellows with us, and we worked the same claim for more than six months."

"I suppose he was quite well?"

"Strong as an ox."

"And—and happy?" pursued the widow, bending closer over her knitting.

"Hum—the less said about that the better, perhaps. But he seemed to enjoy life after a fashion of his own. And he got rich out there, or rather, I will say, well off."

Mrs. Townsend did not pay much attention to that part of the story. Evidently she had not finished asking questions, but she was puzzled about her next one. At last she brought it out beautifully:

"Was his wife with him in California?"

The stranger looked at her with twinkling eyes.

"His wife, ma'am! Why, bless you, he has not got any wife."

"Oh, I thought—I mean I heard"—here the little widow remembered the fate of Ananias and Sapphira, and stopped short before she told such a tremendous fib.

"Whatever you heard of his marrying was all nonsense, I can assure you. I knew him well, and he had no thoughts of the kind about him. Some of the boys used to tease him about it, but he soon made them stop."

"How?"

"He just told them frankly that the only woman he ever loved had jilted him years before,[Pg 219] and married another man. After that no one ever mentioned the subject to him, except me."

Mrs. Townsend laid her knitting aside, and looked thoughtfully into the fire.

"He was another specimen of the class of men I was speaking of. I have seen him face death a score of times as quietly as I face the fire. 'It matters very little what takes me off,' he used to say; 'I've nothing to live for, and there's no one that will shed a tear for me when I am gone.' It's a sad thought for a man to have, isn't it?"

Mrs. Townsend sighed as she said she thought it was.

"But did he ever tell you the name of the woman who jilted him?"

"I know her *first* name."

"What was it?"

"Maria."

The plump little widow almost started out of her chair, the name was spoken so exactly as Sam would have said it.

"Did you know her, too?" he asked, looking keenly at her.

"Yes."

"Intimately?"

"Yes."

"Where is she now? Still happy with her husband, I suppose, and never giving a thought to the poor fellow she drove out into the world?"

"No," said Mrs. Townsend, shading her face with her hand, and speaking unsteadily;"no, her husband is dead."

"Ah! but still she never thinks of Sam."

There was a dead silence.

"Does she?"

"How can I tell?"

"Are you still friends?"

"Yes."

"Then you ought to know, and you do. Tell me."

[Pg 220]

"I'm sure I don't know why I should. But if I do, you must promise me, on your honor, never to tell him, if you ever meet him again."

"Madam, what you say to me never shall be repeated to any mortal man, upon my honor."

"Well, then, she does remember him."

"But how?"

"As kindly, I think, as he could wish."

"I am glad to hear it, for his sake. You and I are the friends of both parties: we can rejoice with each other."

He drew his chair much nearer hers, and took her hand. One moment the widow resisted, but it was a magnetic touch, the rosy palm lay quietly in his, and the dark beard bent so low that it nearly touched her shoulder. It did not matter much. Was he not Samuel's dear friend? If he was not the rose, had he not dwelt very near it, for a long, long time?

"It was a foolish quarrel that parted them," said the stranger, softly.

"Did he tell you about it?"

"Yes, on board the whaler."

"Did he blame her much?"

"Not so much as himself. He said that his jealousy and ill-temper drove her to break off the match; but he thought sometimes if he had only gone back and spoken kindly to her, she would have married him after all."

"I am sure she would," said the widow piteously. "She has owned it to me more than a thousand times."

"She was not happy, then, with another."

"Mr.—that is to say, her husband—was very good and kind," said the little woman, thinking of the lonely grave out on the hillside rather penitently, "and they lived very pleasantly together. There never was a harsh word between them."

"Still—might she not have been happier with Sam? Be honest, now, and say just what you think."

"Yes."

"Bravo! that is what I wanted to come at. And now I have a secret to tell you, and you must break it to her."

Mrs. Townsend looked rather scared.

"What is it?"

"I want you to go and see her, wherever she may be, and say to her, 'Maria,'—what makes you start so?"

"Nothing; only you speak so like some one I used to know, once in a while."

"Do I? Well, take the rest of the message. Tell her that Sam loved her through the whole; that, when he heard she was free, he began to work hard at making a fortune. He has got it; and he is coming to share it with her, if she will let him. Will you tell her this?"

The widow did not answer. She had freed her hand from his, and covered her face with it. By and by she looked up again—he was waiting patiently.

"Well?"

"I will tell her."

He rose from his seat, and walked up and down the room. Then he came back, and leaning on the mantel-piece, stroked the yellow hide of Bose with his slipper.

"Make her quite understand that he wants her for his wife. She may live where she likes and how she likes, only it must be with him."

"I will tell her."

"Say he has grown old, but not cold; that he loves her now perhaps better than he did twenty years ago; that he has been faithful to her all through his life, and that he will be faithful till he dies."

The Californian broke off suddenly. The widow answered still, "I will tell her."

"And what do you think she will say?" he asked, in an altered tone.

"What *can* she say but *Come*!"

"Hurrah!"

The stranger caught her out of her chair as if she had been a child, and kissed her.

"Don't—oh, don't!" she cried out. "I am Sam's Maria!"

"Well—I am Maria's Sam!"

Off went the dark wig and the black whiskers—there smiled the dear face she had not forgotten! I leave you to imagine the tableau; even the cat got up to look, and Bose sat on his stump of a tail, and wondered if he was on his heels or his head.

The widow gave one little scream, and then she—

But, stop! Quiet people like you and me, dear reader, who have got over all these follies, and can do nothing but turn up our noses at them, have no business here. I will only add that two hearts were very happy, that Bose concluded after a while that all was right, and so lay down to sleep again, and that one week afterward, on Christmas Eve, there was a wedding at the house that made the neighbors stare. The widow had married her First Love!

THE SONG OF THE STAR

By C.H. Mead

"Oh, boys; you can count me out on that—all I can get goes to my mother and sisters for Christmas."

The speaker was a manly little newsboy, with good features, a clean face and bright eyes. His clothes looked neat, though they were adorned with numerous patches.

"But see here, Will. Christmas only comes once a year, and why shouldn't we fellers have our banquet as well as the silk-stockings? What would they know about things going on in the world anyway, if we newsboys didn't supply 'em with papers? All in favor of having a banquet, hold up yer hands!"

Up went a score of hands—some dirty, some clean and some speckled, but Will's hand remained down. "See here, Will, what's the reason you won't stay by us?"

The boy hesitated a moment and then said: "Boys, it's mighty close times up at our house; fried chicken and pound cake don't come our way, turkeys roost too high for us, and, and—well, boys, if you must know it, about the only good thing we kids have up there is our mother's love. See these patches! My mother put them on. See these stockings! My mother has been mending this same pair of stockings for more than a year, and she washes and irons them after I've gone to bed at night. Every stitch of mother's needle and thread is a stitch of love, and one night not long ago, I opened my eyes and saw my mother's tears[Pg 245] dropping on the sleeve of my coat at the same time she was putting the patch on this elbow. I tell you, boys, the best thing I've got in the world is my mother, and the best Christmas gift I ever had is my mother's love. If I had a million dollars, I'd give them all to my mother in return for her love. No, no, boys; no banquet for me, as long as I know my mother is starving herself that we children may have more to eat."

"Well," replied one of the boys, "if I had a mother like that, maybe I'd feel the same way; but all we get at our house is a good licking from a drunken mother, and I'm going in for a square meal at Christmas, if I never has another."

The boys, gathered on the sidewalk by one of the parks, were suddenly startled by a cry "Look out there!" and the next moment a runaway horse dashed into their midst; little Will was knocked over, and was soon carried into a neighboring drug store, all unconscious of what had happened. It was soon discovered that his arm was broken, and his body bruised in a number of places. The moment he regained consciousness and found what had occurred, he said:

"Take me to my mother; she will take care of me somehow, though this isn't exactly the kind of a Christmas gift I meant she should have. Say, boys, one of you go up to our house, and tell her easy about this; don't burst in sudden and scare her, but tell her it isn't dangerous, and—well, just tell her I love her."

The boys wiped their eyes and one of them said, "This busts up our banquet, fellers; I'll go and tell Will's mother, and, say, fellers, shan't I tell her we will give our banquet money to help her out at Christmas?"

A hearty "You bet we will," was the response, as big Tom sped away to carry the news to Will's mother, while kind hands helped carry the injured[Pg 246] boy to his home. It was a poor home into which he was borne, but everything was as neat and tidy as could be. A woman stood at the door, and it needed but one glance to know that she was the mother of Will. Poverty and hunger had failed to rob her of her beauty, and there was an air of refinement about her that told of better days and happier surroundings.

"Christmas hasn't come yet, mother," said Will, "but I have. Don't you worry; I'll come out of this all right, and we will have a good Christmas yet."

The mother kissed him tenderly as she said, "No, I will not worry, so long as I have God, and you, and Josie, and Maggie, and Tot. When Christmas comes round, Will, it will be a good day whatever it brings."

"It will bring yer heaps of things, Mrs. Sandford," blurted out big Tom, "for we fellers has given up havin' a banquet, and are going to bring yer something that Will can't bring now. Don't yer worry a bit," and here the rough fellow burst into tears, and rushed out of the house.

A few more days, and then Christmas Eve came round, and a bright night it was. Will lay sleeping on the bed, his mother near by, pretending to read, but in reality using the dear old Bible as a shield to hide the tears that trickled down her cheeks. The mother was thinking, and thinking fast, too. It was only a little over thirteen years since her father had closed the door in her face and told her never to return. The man she loved was not the fashionable fop her father had selected for her as a husband, and secretly she had given her hand to the man to whom long before she had given her heart. All went well, until three years ago, when her husband died suddenly, and she found herself with no means and four children to take care of. Too proud to apply to her father for[Pg 247] help, she struggled on as best she could, leaning hard on the God whom her mother had taught her to love.

Her children were a comfort to her, for they had inherited the natural goodness of both their parents. Her tears now fell fast, for as she thought, she also listened to the voices of her two youngest children who were standing over by the window together.

"Say, Maggie, does yer see dat bright star up dere? I wonder if dat is de star what de shepherds seen! If it is, it seems to be looking right down at us. Maybe Jesus is in dat star, and if He is, He won't forget us, will He?"

And Tot looked at Maggie as the latter said: "Jesus loved little children, Tot, when He was on the earth, and I guess He loves them yet. That's a very bright star—it must be the one that was seen by the shepherds at Bethlehem."

"I think so, too," said Tot, "and may be Josie will hear some of dem 'good tidings' while she is out. Oh!

Maggie, Jesus must love mother; she is so good, and I think He has sent that star to tell us to look out for good news."

And where was Josie all this time? The mother thought she had gone into a neighbor's, where she frequently went, and so felt no anxiety.

Out in the streets of the big city, side by side walked plenty and poverty, wealth and wretchedness, happiness and hunger, gladness and grief. Some carried bundles in their arms, while others carried burdens in their hearts. Over all, the good God watched, and down upon all the bright star shone. But what is that? Suddenly on one of the streets the people stopped and listened. On the steps of a stoop leading up to a lighted mansion stood a little girl who looked like a bright angel from heaven. Far above, overhead, shone the bright star that Maggie and Tot had seen; it was their[Pg 248] star and it was her star, for Josie, too, had discovered it, and somehow felt that the star that had brought "good tidings of great joy" to the shepherds on Bethlehem's plains, had come again and to bring once more "good tidings." She had mounted the steps to get nearer the star, and then all unconscious of the people, in a rich, sweet voice, she sang:—

I think, when I read that sweet story of old,
When Jesus was here among men;
How He called little children, as lambs to His fold;
I should like to have been with Him then.
I wish that His hands had been placed on my head,
That His arms had been thrown around me;

That I might have seen His kind look, when He said,
"Let the little ones come unto Me."

As she sang, her gaze was fixed on the star, and even her hands were lifted toward it. The people looked at her; an angel had appeared in their midst—her face, her voice, her upturned eyes, her uplifted hands, held them spell-bound, until some one looking up in the direction she pointed, cried out: "See that star!" Heavenward went the gaze of the multitude, and once more there seemed to come to them a voice, saying: "Fear not, for behold I bring you good tidings of great joy, which shall be to all people." The face of Josie was illumined and even the multitude that had gathered, failed to alarm her. The star with its "good tidings" was over her head and in her heart as well. "Who are you, my child?" said a gentleman who had come up on the steps where she stood. "Please, sir, I am Josie Sandford." The gentleman gave a start and said, "Sandford, Josie Sandford? Pray where do you live, Josie?" She told him, and in[Pg 249] response to other questions, told of mother, brother and sisters.

"Oh, sir; do you see the star? I am sure it has some 'good tidings' for us at our house, and I must hurry home and tell mother all about it. Good-bye."

Away sped the child until she reached her home, and then entering the room quietly, she went up to her mother and said: "Have you seen the star, mother?" Maggie and Tot cried out, "We've seen it; come, mother, and look quick." The mother went quietly to the window, and there beheld a star of wonderful brightness, and as she gazed, her face took on a new light and into her heart came a great peace. The sleeping boy was awakened by the voices, and he, too, made his way to the window and looked at the star. "At evening time it shall be light."

It had come, and—something else had come, too, for steps were heard on the stairs, followed by a knock on the door, on opening which, in came a company of newsboys headed by big Tom. They bore bundles and baskets, provisions and poultry, sunshine and sugar, toys and turnips, good-will and grapes, cheer and celery, and things that no one but those who had lacked for them, would ever have thought of. Big Tom was the spokesman for the happy company.

"If yer please, Mrs. Sandford," he said, "there's our banquet. We wasn't going to come until to-morrow morning, but when we got the things all together, we just couldn't wait any longer, so we've brought 'em to-night, and if it isn't too soon, ma'am, we wishes you, and Will, and Josie, and Maggie, and Tot a 'Merry Christmas,' doesn't we, boys?"

"Indeed we does!" responded the boys. The faces of that mother and her children were a sight to behold. Smiles and tears greeted the boys, and[Pg 250] the mother and her three girls had a kiss for each of them. Then Tot said: "I knowed it. I knowed it! De star had Jesus in it, and I knowed He see Maggie and me looking up at it."

"Well, boys," said Mrs. Sandford, "you shall have your banquet, for I want you all to take Christmas dinner with us to-morrow."

"Yes, boys, you shall all take dinner with Mrs. Sandford and her children to-morrow, but it must be at the home of her parents and not here," said a gentleman who had not been noticed as he stood in the hallway.

Mrs. Sandford started as the owner of the voice entered the room, and little Josie sprang toward him at the same moment. She resembled her mother and was her namesake as well. The gentleman stretched out his arms toward Mrs. Sandford as he said to her:

"Josie, can you forgive me for the harshness with which I drove you years ago from my door? God only knows how I have suffered, and for years I have hunted high and low for you, and have advertised time and again. But all was in vain, until to-night I saw your face and heard your voice once more, as my grandchild, Josie, stood singing on the steps and gazing at the star. In her I found you again, and oh, how your mother and I have prayed for this time to come."

Long before he had finished, the daughter was in her father's arms once more, and the children were clinging to their new-found grandparent. The newsboys looked on in wonder, and suddenly little Tot ran to the window and then cried out—"Oh, grandpa, the star is here yet, and it shines brighter than before," and she threw a kiss up to the star.

Christmas morning came and found them all in a home of plenty. A chair that had long stood vacant at that table, was once more filled, and near[Pg 251] it were four other chairs for the new-found grandchildren. Was it a "Merry Christmas," did you inquire? Just ask those newsboys who came at two o'clock if they ever had such a banquet before or since, or whether they ever saw a home in which the "Star of Bethlehem" shone with greater splendor. And over the earth the star still shines, and will continue to shine until all mankind shall yet have a "Merry Christmas."

My Christmas Dinner

By Anonymous

It was on the twentieth of December last that I received an invitation from my friend, Mr. Phiggins, to dine with him in Mark Lane, on Christmas Day. I had several reasons for declining this proposition. The first was that Mr. P. makes it a rule, at all these festivals, to empty the entire contents of his counting-house into his little dining parlor; and you consequently sit down to dinner with six white-waistcoated clerks, let loose upon a turkey. The second was that I am not sufficiently well read in cotton and sugar, to enter with any spirit into the subject of conversation. And the third was, and is, that I never drink Cape wine. But by far the most prevailing reason remains to be told. I had been anticipating for some days, and was hourly in the hope of receiving, an invitation to spend my Christmas Day in a most irresistible quarter. I was expecting, indeed, the felicity of eating plum-pudding with an angel; and, on the strength of my imaginary engagement, I returned a polite note to Mr. P., reducing him to the necessity of advertising for another candidate for Cape and turkey.

The twenty-first came. Another invitation—to dine with a regiment of roast-beef eaters, at Clapham. I declined this also, for the above reason, and for one other, *viz.*, that, on dining there ten Christmas Days ago, it was discovered, on sitting down, that one little accompaniment of the roast beef had been entirely overlooked. Would it be believed!—but I will not stay to mystify—I merely mention the fact. They had forgotten the horseradish.

The next day arrived, and with it a neat epistle, sealed with violet-colored wax, from Upper Brook street. "Dine with the ladies—at home on Christmas Day." Very tempting, it is true; but not exactly the letter I was longing for. I began, however, to debate within myself upon the policy of securing this bird in hand, instead of waiting for the two that were still hopping about the bush, when the consultation was suddenly brought to a close, by a prophetic view of the portfolio of drawings fresh from boarding-school—moths and roses on embossed paper;—to say nothing of the album, in which I stood engaged to write an elegy on a Java sparrow, that had been the favorite in the family for three days. I rung for gilt-edged, pleaded a world of polite regret, and again declined.

The twenty-third dawned; time was getting on rather rapidly; but no card came. I began to despair of any more invitations, and to repent of my refusals. Breakfast was hardly over, however, when the servant brought up—not a letter—but an aunt and a brace of cousins from Bayswater. They would listen to no excuse; consanguinity required me, and Christmas was not my own. Now my cousins kept no albums; they are really as pretty as cousins can be; and when violent hands, with white kid gloves, are laid on one, it is sometimes difficult to effect an escape with becoming elegance. I could not, however, give up my darling hope of a pleasanter prospect. They fought with me in fifty engagements—that I pretended to have made. I showed them the Court Guide, with ten names obliterated—being those of persons who had *not* asked me to mince-meat and mistletoe; and I ultimately gained my cause by quartering the remains of an infectious fever on the sensitive fears of my aunt, and by dividing a rheumatism and a sprained ankle between my sympathetic cousins.

The Elves and the Shoemaker

By Horace E. Scudder

There was once a shoemaker who worked very hard and was honest. Still, he could not earn enough to live on. At last, all he had in the world was gone except just leather enough to make one pair of shoes. He cut these out at night, and meant to rise early the next morning to make them up.

His heart was light in spite of his troubles, for his conscience was clear. So he went quietly to bed, left all his cares to God, and fell asleep. In the morning he said his prayers, and sat down to work, when, to his great wonder, there stood the shoes, already made, upon the table.

The good man knew not what to say or think. He looked at the work. There was not one false stitch in the whole job. All was neat and true.

That same day a customer came in, and the shoes pleased him so well that he readily paid a price higher than usual for them. The shoemaker took the money and bought leather enough to make two pairs more. He cut out the work in the evening, and went to bed early. He wished to be up with the sun and get to work.

He was saved all trouble, for when he got up in the morning, the work was done. Pretty soon buyers came in, who paid him well for his goods. So he bought leather enough for four pairs more.

He cut out the work again overnight, and found it finished in the morning as before. So it went on for some time. What was got ready at night was always done by daybreak, and the good man soon was well-to-do.

One evening, at Christmas-time, he and his wife sat over the fire, chatting, and he said: "I should like to sit up and watch to-night, that we may see who it is that comes and does my work for me." So they left the light burning, and hid themselves behind a curtain to see what would happen.

As soon as it was midnight, there came two little Elves. They sat upon the shoemaker's bench, took up all the work that was cut out, and began to ply their little fingers. They stitched and rapped and tapped at such a rate that the shoemaker was amazed, and could not take his eyes off them for a moment.

On they went till the job was done, and the shoes stood, ready for use, upon the table. This was long before daybreak. Then they ran away as quick as lightning.

The next day the wife said to the shoemaker: "These little Elves have made us rich, and we ought to be thankful to them, and do them some good in return. I am vexed to see them run about as they do. They have nothing upon their backs to keep off the cold. I'll tell you what we must do. I will make each of them a shirt, and a coat and waistcoat, and a pair of pantaloons into the bargain. Do you make each of them a little pair of shoes."

The good shoemaker liked the thought very well. One evening he and his wife had the clothes ready, and laid them on the table instead of the work they used to cut out. Then they went and hid behind the curtain to watch what the little Elves would do.

At midnight the Elves came in and were going to sit down at their work as usual. But when they saw the clothes lying there for them, they laughed and were in high glee. They dressed themselves in the twinkling of an eye, and danced and capered and sprang about as merry as could be, till at last they danced out of the door, and over the green.

The shoemaker saw them no more, but everything went well with him as long as he lived.

The Christmas Fairy of Strasburg

by J. Stirling Coyne

A German Folk-Tale

Once, long ago, there lived near the ancient city of Strasburg, on the river Rhine, a young and handsome count, whose name was Otto. As the years flew by he remained unwed, and never so much as cast a glance at the fair maidens of the country round; for this reason people began to call him "Stone-Heart."

It chanced that Count Otto, on one Christmas Eve, ordered that a great hunt should take place in the forest surrounding his castle. He and his guests and his many retainers rode forth, and the chase became more and more exciting. It led through thickets, and over pathless tracts of forest, until at length Count Otto found himself separated from his companions.

He rode on by himself until he came to a spring of clear, bubbling water, known to the people around as the "Fairy Well." Here Count Otto dismounted. He bent over the spring and began to lave his hands in the sparkling tide, but to his wonder he found that though the weather was cold and frosty, the water was warm and delightfully caressing. He felt a glow of joy pass through his veins, and, as he plunged his hands deeper, he fancied that his right hand was grasped by another, soft and small, which gently slipped from his finger the gold ring he always wore. And, lo! when he drew out his hand, the gold ring was gone.

Full of wonder at this mysterious event, the count mounted his horse and returned to his castle, resolving in his mind that the very next day he would have the Fairy Well emptied by his servants.

He retired to his room, and, throwing himself just as he was upon his couch, tried to sleep; but the strangeness of the adventure kept him restless and wakeful.

Suddenly he heard the hoarse baying of the watch-hounds in the courtyard, and then the creaking of the drawbridge, as though it were being lowered. Then came to his ear the patter of many small feet on the stone staircase, and next he heard indistinctly the sound of light footsteps in the chamber adjoining his own.

Count Otto sprang from his couch, and as he did so there sounded a strain of delicious music, and the door of his chamber was flung open. Hurrying into the next room, he found himself in the midst of numberless Fairy beings, clad in gay and sparkling robes. They paid no heed to him, but began to dance, and laugh, and sing, to the sound of mysterious music.

In the center of the apartment stood a splendid Christmas Tree, the first ever seen in that country. Instead of toys and candles there hung on its lighted boughs diamond stars, pearl necklaces, bracelets of gold ornamented with colored jewels, aigrettes of rubies and sapphires, silken belts embroidered with Oriental pearls, and daggers mounted in gold and studded with the rarest gems. The whole tree swayed, sparkled, and glittered in the radiance of its many lights.

Count Otto stood speechless, gazing at all this wonder, when suddenly the Fairies stopped dancing and fell back, to make room for a lady of dazzling beauty who came slowly toward him.

She wore on her raven-black tresses a golden diadem set with jewels. Her hair flowed down upon a robe of rosy satin and creamy velvet. She stretched out two small, white hands to the count and addressed him in sweet, alluring tones:—

"Dear Count Otto," said she, "I come to return your Christmas visit. I am Ernestine, the Queen of the Fairies. I bring you something you lost in the Fairy Well."

And as she spoke she drew from her bosom a golden casket, set with diamonds, and placed it in his hands. He opened it eagerly and found within his lost gold ring.

Carried away by the wonder of it all, and overcome by an irresistible impulse, the count pressed the Fairy Ernestine to his heart, while she, holding him by the hand, drew him into the magic mazes of the dance. The mysterious music floated through the room, and the rest of that Fairy company circled and whirled around the Fairy Queen and Count Otto, and then gradually dissolved into a mist of many colors, leaving the count and his beautiful guest alone.

Then the young man, forgetting all his former coldness toward the maidens of the country round about, fell on his knees before the Fairy and besought her to become his bride. At last she consented on the condition that he should never speak the word "death" in her presence.

The next day the wedding of Count Otto and Ernestine, Queen of the Fairies, was celebrated with great pomp and magnificence, and the two continued to live happily for many years.

Now it happened on a time, that the count and his Fairy wife were to hunt in the forest around the castle. The horses were saddled and bridled, and standing at the door, the company waited, and the count paced the hall in great impatience; but still the Fairy Ernestine tarried long in her chamber. At length she appeared at the door of the hall, and the count addressed her in anger.

"You have kept us waiting so long," he cried, "that you would make a good messenger to send for Death!"

Scarcely had he spoken the forbidden and fatal word, when the Fairy, uttering a wild cry, vanished from his sight. In vain Count Otto, overwhelmed with grief and remorse, searched the castle and the Fairy Well, no trace could he find of his beautiful, lost wife but the imprint of her delicate hand set in the stone arch above the castle gate.

Years passed by, and the Fairy Ernestine did not return. The count continued to grieve. Every Christmas Eve he set up a lighted tree in the room where he had first met the Fairy, hoping in vain that she would return to him.

Time passed and the count died. The castle fell into ruins. But to this day may be seen above the massive gate, deeply sunken in the stone arch, the impress of a small and delicate hand.

And such, say the good folk of Strasburg, was the origin of the Christmas Tree.

VANKA

By Anton P. Chekhov

Nine-year-old Vanka Zhukov, who had been apprentice to the shoemaker Aliakhin for three months, did not go to bed the night before Christmas. He waited till the master and mistress and the assistants had gone out to an early church-service, to procure from his employer's cupboard a small phial of ink and a penholder with a rusty nib; then, spreading a crumpled sheet of paper in front of him, he began to write.

Before, however, deciding to make the first letter, he looked furtively at the door and at the window, glanced several times at the sombre ikon, on either side of which stretched shelves full of lasts, and heaved a heart-rending sigh. The sheet of paper was spread on a bench, and he himself was on his knees in front of it.

"Dear Grandfather Konstantin Makarych," he wrote, "I am writing you a letter. I wish you a Happy Christmas and all God's holy best. I have no mamma or papa, you are all I have."

Vanka gave a look towards the window in which shone the reflection of his candle, and vividly pictured to himself his grandfather, Konstantin Makarych, who was night-watchman at Messrs. Zhivarev. He was a small, lean, unusually lively and active old man of sixty-five, always smiling and blear-eyed. All day he slept in the servants' kitchen or trifled with the cooks. At night, enveloped in an ample sheep-skin coat, he strayed round the domain tapping with his cudgel. Behind him, each hanging its head, walked the old bitch Kashtanka, and the dog Viun, so named because of his black coat and long body and his resemblance to a loach. Viun was an unusually civil and friendly dog, looking as kindly at a stranger as at his masters, but he was not to be trusted. Beneath his deference and humbleness was hid the most inquisitorial maliciousness. No one knew better than he how to sneak up and take a bite at a leg, or slip into the larder or steal a muzhik's chicken. More than once they had nearly broken his hind-legs, twice he had been hung up, every week he was nearly flogged to death, but he always recovered.

At this moment, for certain, Vanka's grandfather must be standing at the gate, blinking his eyes at the bright red windows of the village church, stamping his feet in their high-felt boots, and jesting with the people in the yard; his cudgel will be hanging from his belt, he will be hugging himself with cold, giving a little dry, old man's cough, and at times pinching a servant-girl or a cook.

"Won't we take some snuff?" he asks, holding out his snuff-box to the women. The women take a pinch of snuff, and sneeze.

The old man goes into indescribable ecstasies, breaks into loud laughter, and cries:

"Off with it, it will freeze to your nose!"

He gives his snuff to the dogs, too. Kashtanka sneezes, twitches her nose, and walks away offended. Viun deferentially refuses to sniff and wags his tail. It is glorious weather, not a breath of wind, clear, and frosty; it is a dark night, but the whole village, its white roofs and streaks of smoke from the chimneys, the trees silvered with hoar-frost, and the snowdrifts, you can see it all. The sky scintillates with bright twinkling stars, and the Milky Way stands out so clearly that it looks as if it had been polished and rubbed over with snow for the holidays...

Vanka sighs, dips his pen in the ink, and continues to write:

"Last night I got a thrashing, my master dragged me by my hair into the yard, and belaboured me with a shoe-maker's stirrup, because, while I was rocking his brat in its cradle, I unfortunately fell asleep. And during the week, my mistress told me to clean a herring, and I began by its tail, so she took the herring and stuck its snout into my face. The assistants tease me, send me to the tavern for vodka, make me steal the master's cucumbers, and the master beats me with whatever is handy. Food there is none; in the morning it's bread, at dinner gruel, and in the evening bread again. As for tea or sour-cabbage soup, the master and the mistress themselves guzzle that. They make me sleep in the vestibule, and when their brat cries, I don't sleep at all, but have to rock the cradle. Dear Grandpapa, for Heaven's sake, take me away from here, home to our village, I can't bear this any more... I bow to the ground to you, and will pray to God for ever and ever, take me from here or I shall die..."

The corners of Vanka's mouth went down, he rubbed his eyes with his dirty fist, and sobbed.

"I'll grate your tobacco for you," he continued, "I'll pray to God for you, and if there is anything wrong, then flog me like the grey goat. And if you really think I shan't find work, then I'll ask the manager, for Christ's sake, to let me clean the boots, or I'll go instead of Fedya as underherdsman. Dear Grandpapa, I can't bear this any more, it'll kill me... I wanted to run away to our village, but I have no boots, and I was afraid of the frost, and when I grow up I'll look after you, no one shall harm you, and when you die I'll pray for the repose of your soul, just like I do for mamma Pelagueya.

"As for Moscow, it is a large town, there are all gentlemen's houses, lots of horses, no sheep, and the dogs are not vicious. The children don't come round at Christmas with a star, no one is allowed to sing in the choir, and once I saw in a shop window hooks on a line and fishing rods, all for sale, and for every kind of fish, awfully convenient. And there was one hook which would catch a sheat-fish weighing a pound. And there are shops with guns, like the master's, and I am sure they must cost 100 rubles each. And in the meat-shops there are woodcocks, partridges, and hares, but who shot them or where they come from, the shopman won't say.

"Dear Grandpapa, and when the masters give a Christmas tree, take a golden walnut and hide it in my green box. Ask the young lady, Olga Ignatyevna, for it, say it's for Vanka."

Vanka sighed convulsively, and again stared at the window. He remembered that his grandfather always went to the forest for the Christmas tree, and took his grandson with him. What happy times! The frost crackled, his grandfather crackled, and as they both did, Vanka did the same. Then before cutting down the Christmas tree his grandfather smoked his pipe, took a long pinch of snuff, and made fun of poor frozen little Vanka... The young fir trees, wrapt in hoar-frost, stood motionless, waiting for which of them would die. Suddenly a hare springing from somewhere would dart over the snowdrift... His grandfather could not help shouting:

"Catch it, catch it, catch it! Ah, short-tailed devil!"

When the tree was down, his grandfather dragged it to the master's house, and there they set about decorating it. The young lady, Olga Ignatyevna, Vanka's great friend, busied herself most about it. When little Vanka's mother, Pelagueya, was still alive, and was servant-woman in the house, Olga Ignatyevna used to stuff him with sugar-candy, and, having nothing to do, taught him to read, write, count up to one hundred, and even to dance the quadrille. When Pelagueya died, they placed the orphan Vanka in the kitchen with his grandfather, and from the kitchen he was sent to Moscow to Aliakhin, the shoemaker.

"Come quick, dear Grandpapa," continued Vanka, "I beseech you for Christ's sake take me from here. Have pity on a poor orphan, for here they beat me, and I am frightfully hungry, and so sad that I can't tell you, I cry all the time. The other day the master hit me on the head with a last; I fell to the ground, and only just returned to life. My life is a misfortune, worse than any dog's... I send greetings to Aliona, to one-eyed Tegor, and the coachman, and don't let any one have my mouth-organ. I remain, your grandson, Ivan Zhukov, dear Grandpapa, do come."

Vanka folded his sheet of paper in four, and put it into an envelope purchased the night before for a kopek. He thought a little, dipped the pen into the ink, and wrote the address:

"The village, to my grandfather." He then scratched his head, thought again, and added: "Konstantin Makarych." Pleased at not having been interfered with in his writing, he put on his cap, and, without putting on his sheep-skin coat, ran out in his shirt-sleeves into the street.

The shopman at the poulterer's, from whom he had inquired the night before, had told him that letters were to be put into post-boxes, and from there they were conveyed over the whole earth in mail troikas by drunken post-boys and to the sound of bells. Vanka ran to the first post-box and slipped his precious letter into the slit.

An hour afterwards, lulled by hope, he was sleeping soundly. In his dreams he saw a stove, by the stove his grandfather sitting with his legs dangling down, barefooted, and reading a letter to the cooks, and Viun walking round the stove wagging his tail.

The Heavenly Christmas Tree

By Fyodor Dostoevsky

I am a novelist, and I suppose I have made up this story. I write "I suppose," though I know for a fact that I have made it up, but yet I keep fancying that it must have happened somewhere at some time, that it must have happened on Christmas Eve in some great town in a time of terrible frost.

I have a vision of a boy, a little boy, six years old or even younger. This boy woke up that morning in a cold damp cellar. He was dressed in a sort of little dressing-gown and was shivering with cold. There was a cloud of white steam from his breath, and sitting on a box in the corner, he blew the steam out of his mouth and amused himself in his dullness watching it float away. But he was terribly hungry. Several times that morning he went up to the plank bed where his sick mother was lying on a mattress as thin as a pancake, with some sort of bundle under her head for a pillow. How had she come here? She must have come with her boy from some other town and suddenly fallen ill. The landlady who let the "corners" had been taken two days before to the police station, the lodgers were out and about as the holiday was so near, and the only one left had been lying for the last twenty-four hours dead drunk, not having waited for Christmas. In another corner of the room a wretched old woman of eighty, who had once been a children's nurse but was now left to die friendless, was moaning and groaning with rheumatism, scolding and grumbling at the boy so that he was afraid to go near her corner. He had got a drink of water in the outer room, but could not find a crust anywhere, and had been on the point of waking his mother a dozen times. He felt frightened at last in the darkness: it had long[152] been dusk, but no light was kindled. Touching his mother's face, he was surprised that she did not move at all, and that she was as cold as the wall. "It is very cold here," he thought. He stood a little, unconsciously letting his hands rest on the dead woman's shoulders, then he breathed on his fingers to warm them, and then quietly fumbling for his cap on the bed, he went out of the cellar. He would have gone earlier, but was afraid of the big dog which had been howling all day at the neighbour's door at the top of the stairs. But the dog was not there now, and he went out into the street.

Mercy on us, what a town! He had never seen anything like it before. In the town from which he had come, it was always such black darkness at night. There was one lamp for the whole street, the little, low-pitched, wooden houses were closed up with shutters, there was no one to be seen in the street after dusk, all the people shut themselves up in their houses, and there was nothing but the howling of packs of dogs, hundreds and thousands of them barking and howling all night. But there it was so warm and he was given food, while here—oh, dear, if he only had something to eat! And what a noise and rattle here, what light and what people, horses and carriages, and what a frost! The frozen steam hung in clouds over the horses, over their warmly breathing mouths; their hoofs clanged against the stones through the powdery snow, and every one pushed so, and—oh, dear, how he longed for some morsel to eat, and how wretched he suddenly felt. A policeman walked by and turned away to avoid seeing the boy.

Here was another street—oh, what a wide one, here he would be run over for certain; how everyone was shouting, racing and driving along, and the light, the light! And what was this? A huge glass window, and through the window a tree reaching up to the ceiling; it was a fir tree, and on it were ever so many lights, gold papers and apples and little dolls and horses; and there were children clean and dressed[153] in their best running about the room, laughing and playing and eating and drinking something. And then a little girl began dancing with one of the boys, what a pretty little girl! And he could hear the music through the window. The boy looked and wondered and laughed, though his toes were aching with the cold and his fingers were red and stiff so that it hurt him to move them. And all at once the boy remembered how his toes and fingers hurt him, and began crying, and ran on; and again through another window-pane he saw another Christmas tree, and on a table cakes of all sorts—almond cakes, red cakes and yellow cakes, and three grand young ladies were sitting there, and they gave the cakes to any one who went up to them, and the door kept opening, lots of gentlemen and ladies went in from the street. The boy crept up, suddenly opened the door and went in. Oh, how they shouted at him and waved him back! One lady went up to him hurriedly and slipped a kopeck into his hand, and with her own hands opened the door into the street for him! How frightened he was. And the kopeck rolled away and clinked upon the steps; he could not bend his red fingers to hold it tight. The boy ran away and went on, where he did not know. He was ready to cry again but he was afraid, and ran on and on and blew his fingers. And he was miserable because he felt suddenly so lonely and terrified, and all at once, mercy on us! What was this again? People were standing in a crowd admiring. Behind a glass window there were three little dolls, dressed in red and green dresses, and exactly, exactly as though they were alive. One was a little old man sitting and playing a big violin, the two others were standing close by and playing little violins and nodding in time, and looking at one another, and their lips moved, they were speaking, actually speaking, only one couldn't hear through the glass. And at first the boy thought they were alive, and when he grasped that they were dolls he laughed. He had never seen such dolls before, and had no idea there were such[154] dolls! And he wanted to cry, but he felt amused, amused by the dolls. All at once he fancied that some one caught at his smock behind: a wicked big boy was standing beside him and suddenly hit him on the head, snatched off his cap and tripped him up. The boy fell down on the ground, at once there was a shout, he was numb with fright, he jumped up and ran away. He ran, and not knowing where he was going, ran in at the gate of some one's courtyard, and sat down behind a stack of wood: "They won't find me here, besides it's dark!"

He sat huddled up and was breathless from fright, and all at once, quite suddenly, he felt so happy: his hands and feet suddenly left off aching and grew so warm, as warm as though he were on a stove; then he shivered all over, then he gave a start, why, he must have been asleep. How nice to have a sleep here! "I'll sit here a little and go and look at the dolls again," said the boy, and smiled thinking of them. "Just as though they were alive!..." And suddenly he heard his mother singing over him. "Mammy, I am asleep; how nice it is to sleep here!"

"Come to my Christmas tree, little one," a soft voice suddenly whispered over his head.

He thought that this was still his mother, but no, it was not she. Who it was calling him, he could not see, but some one bent over and embraced him in the darkness; and he stretched out his hands to him, and ... and all at once—oh, what a bright light! Oh, what a Christmas tree! And yet it was not a fir tree, he had never seen a tree like that! Where was he now? Everything was bright and shining, and all round him were dolls; but no, they were not dolls, they were little boys and girls, only so bright and shining. They all came flying round him, they all kissed him, took him and carried him along with them, and he was flying himself, and he saw that his mother was looking at him and laughing joyfully. "Mammy, Mammy; oh, how nice it is here, Mammy!" And again he kissed the children and wanted to tell them at[155] once of those dolls in the shop window. "Who are you, boys? Who are you, girls?" he asked, laughing and admiring them.

"This is Christ's Christmas tree," they answered. "Christ always has a Christmas tree on this day, for the little children who have no tree of their own...." And he found out that all these little boys and girls were children just like himself; that some had been frozen in the baskets in which they had as babies been laid on the doorsteps of well-to-do Petersburg people, others had been boarded out with Finnish women by the Foundling and had been suffocated, others had died at their starved mother's breasts (in the Samara famine), others had died in the third-class railway carriages from the foul air; and yet they were all here, they were all like angels about Christ, and He was in the midst of them and held out His hands to them and blessed them and their sinful mothers.... And the mothers of these children stood on one side weeping; each one knew her boy or girl, and the children flew up to them and kissed them and wiped away their tears with their little hands, and begged them not to weep because they were so happy.

And down below in the morning the porter found the little dead body of the frozen child on the woodstack; they sought out his mother too.... She had died before him. They met before the Lord God in heaven.

Why have I made up such a story, so out of keeping with an ordinary diary, and a writer's above all? And I promised two stories dealing with real events! But that is just it, I keep fancying that all this may have happened really—that is, what took place in the cellar and on the woodstack; but as for Christ's Christmas tree, I cannot tell you whether that could have happened or not.

www.ingramcontent.com/pod-product-compliance
Lightning Source LLC
Chambersburg PA
CBHW050850190726
48286CB00007B/2305

* 9 7 8 1 9 5 3 2 7 9 1 2 5 *